BLAQUE

STREET CHRONICLES

Published by:

G Street Chronicles
P.O. Box 1822
Jonesboro, GA 30237-1822

www.gstreetchronicles.com
fans@gstreetchronicles.com

Cover design:
Hot Book Covers
www.hotbookcovers.com

ISBN: 978-1-9384423-5-3
LCCN: 2012950157

Join us on our social networks
Like us on Facebook
G Street Chronicles Fan Page
G Street Chronicles CEO Exclusive Readers Group

Follow us on Twitter
@GStreetChronicl

Dirty DNA

PROLOGUE

YaSheema, known to the streets simply as YaYa, sat thinking to herself, *Who said pimpin' ain't easy?*

Shit, I wasn't doing half bad for a black woman living in the mean streets of DC with a growing empire. Sex, drugs, money and power could all be mine with the roll of the dice. I was taught good game, and sex appeal was all I ever needed to get by in this fucked up world!

I was the bomb! I faced the mirror that was attached to the vanity that stood in the far corner of my lavish room. I admired myself. I was a dime by anyone's standards and no one could tell me I wasn't either. I stood a proud 5'7" with eyes the color of the heavens after a storm. Stormy grey is what I liked to call 'em. My mocha chocolate skin was the kind bitches would pay big money for. My ass was phat and my thighs were thick. I got that fire a nigga could easily fall in love with. I rocked only the hottest shit money could buy.

My father taught me that I was worth only the best. That was what made me run my shit flawlessly. I wasn't what people would stereotype as a "Boss." Your everyday average nigga had no idea

I was street royalty. They just looked at me like I was a stuck up bitch. They probably thought I was tricking with niggas to buy my diamonds and furs. I am sure they thought I was fucking to be privileged enough to travel to the exotic places of the world.

Most niggas wouldn't wanna believe a bitch like me was on the come up and that I did it on my own. Well, not all on my own, I did have the wisdom and teachings of the trillest niggas in the game, my Daddy. He taught me how to make shit happen. He taught me at all costs to win the game – not just finish the game – but to come in first place and devour all those who tried to take me down in the process.

CHAPTER 1

Rock Creek Park
NW Washington, DC

My father told me at an early age that having good game would get me anywhere. My father was my hero. There was nothing that my daddy didn't have; cars, money, women, and the world could be his for the right price. My father was the king of his streets. He was all my brother, Neko, and I knew.

My mother, Christa Reynolds, was just one of the endless one-night affairs my father had to pass the time away. He never trusted women enough to keep them around longer than a month or two. He used them and threw them away like tissue. He tried to dispose of my mother but she wasn't having it! She held on, even though Darnell wanted no parts of her except for what she had between her legs. He used her so good she would do anything to keep him around, which didn't exclude tricking and an endless list of other whorish acts. She had heard all kinds of stories about Darnell's infidelities and sexual escapades. There was even talk about him fucking with Momma's baby sister; but that didn't stop my mother's money-hungry ass. When she found out she was pregnant with me she just knew she had hit pay dirt. My father had other plans for her.

Christa was a beautiful woman. She was what you would call exotic. She stood a proud 5'8"; an olive-toned beauty with long thick legs and an ass to make a nigga cry. She had also been born with alluring grey eyes. She had a sharp short hair cut and would rock the finest shit she could boost from the stores. Darnell knew she was a gold diggin' bitch. Daddy really could not stand her; but the bitch was bad, and she had some killer pussy.

Darnell wasn't bad him damn self. He cleared an even six feet and was the color of ebony. He had the most beautiful smile and would make the panties of women drop with one look. He rarely smiled though, because his jaw was clinched and he always looked as if he were in deep thought. He was always on the grind, and money was his first and only love; next to me of course.

When Christa told him she was pregnant he thought he would strangle her on the spot. He came close to drugging her junkie ass and getting rid of the evidence, but he thought of his baby. He thought of the small piece of him that he could share his world with. He didn't care if it was a girl or boy; as long as his heir was healthy, he wasn't concerned about the sex of the child.

"So, what are you going to do about this Dee?" Christa asked in a confident tone while tapping her foot against the floor. She figured if she came at him hardcore, he would have no choice but to accept her.

"What do you mean what am I going to do about it? Christa, you know what it is. I'll take care of my business, which is my child." He walked out of the room emotionless, with nothing more to say.

Just like that, Christa Reynolds knew she wouldn't have to boost anymore, or fuck any of those disgusting hustlers to keep up with the lifestyle she was accustomed too. She immediately went to her rundown project home in SE, DC and packed her belongings; telling her mother she wasn't ever coming back. Well, at least not if she could help it.

Darnell treated her like gold until June 4, 1986; that's the day I was born. From that day on, my father pretended my mother didn't exist. Christa hoped that Darnell would warm up to her after the birth of their little girl YaSheema. Instead YaYa, as Darnell liked to call her, was his pride and joy. She was the one who he adorned in the latest fashions. She was the one who was shown off to everyone, and Christa was left alone to do whatever she pleased as long as it didn't mean bothering Darnell.

Christa was determined to make him hers though. She tried to make him want her. She even resorted to fucking his best friend to make Darnell notice she was even alive. He hadn't touched her in God only knew how long, and if he had his way, he never would again. He knew of her deceit and betrayal. He knew Christa was a straight rolla' and she would stop at nothing to get what she wanted.

After years of being ignored, Christa started to hate the fact that she had a child. She knew that YaYa was not the real source behind why she felt the way she felt on the inside. She realized that the child was just being used as a pawn to get her out of the way gracefully. Christa didn't know what to think of YaYa since the majority of her time was spent chasing after Darnell, and the other part was spent getting high. Christa barely even knew she had a child to care for. She would take the money Darnell gave her and stash it away to get herself a fix. Life as an addict was all Christa gave a fuck about.

For years, that was the way things went in my home. I never really noticed the beef between my parents because my father always took the time to spoil me rotten. He made sure I didn't have to want for anything and that included wanting my mother to act as such. The storm was sure to come. It was only a matter of time before my mother's borrowed lifestyle would come to a screeching halt like "new shoes" on an Escalade truck.

CHAPTER 2

CFE Night Club
Marlboro Pike
Forestville, MD

"Christa!" Darnell growled, "Get the fuck down here now!"

Christa had become accustomed to the verbal abuse. To tune it out she just got high. When he threatened to toss her out on the streets, she got high. Hell, she got high just because. She didn't even need a reason these days; it had turned from a recreational thing into a serious habit.

"Look bitch, it is time for you to move on!" Darnell snarled between clenched teeth. He had had enough of her. He had just got word from one of his men that Christa was out fucking a rival Kingpin. It was time for her to go! She was causing too many problems and she just wasn't worth it anymore.

At the time I witnessed this confrontation, I was six years old, and my father had done all he could to keep his family unit together. Actually, my father didn't give a fuck about a family unit; all he cared about was me. And that was all that mattered because Momma acted as though she didn't want me around.

"You're a worthless, money hungry, crack head whore. Get

the fuck out of my house!" Darnell fumed. He was so angry that you could see the hatred in his eyes for what his baby mother had become.

"What am I supposed to do? Where the fuck am I supposed to go?" Christa said between her sobs.

Darnell could no longer keep his composure. "I don't give a fuck what you do or where you go, but a car will be here in two hours to get you and your shit out of my house! I am thinking you would want to hurry up and get your things packed because anything you can't take with you, you won't be coming back to get!"

You could almost see the venom my father was spitting. At that moment, I knew my father was a force to be reckoned with. With that, my father grabbed my hand and tried to lead me away from a scene that was likely to escalate. My mother grabbed for my other hand and yanked me violently in the other direction. "If I go, she goes too!" She wept. She knew I was her only ticket into the sweet life and I resented her for always trying to use me to get ahead.

"Daddy, I don't want to go with her." I whined.

"Oh no, there is no way I am leaving my YaYa with a junkie bitch like you. And since when did you become a parent?" Darnell seethed.

My mother couldn't believe the words that were piercing her very soul. She released the grip she had on my wrist and started back up the staircase mumbling under her breath. Momma wasn't crazy; she wasn't going to make too much fuss too loud. She knew the consequences could have been deadly. That was the last I saw of my Momma until several years later.

Christa had no idea where she went wrong. All her life was spent chasing after a man. It didn't matter which man, or who he belonged to. Married with children...it didn't matter as long as she had something to gain by being with him. Dee was the only person she ever loved, and he threw her out on the streets. This is where she tried to pick up the pieces and salvage whatever she had left. After Dee threw her out she had nowhere to go. She ended up becoming a prostitute doing whatever she could to stay high to numb the pain. She hated who she had become, but she was so wrapped up in the game with a pimp who would rather use her as a punching bag than put her out on the stroll.

CHAPTER 3

The Meeting Place
17th and L Street
NW Washington, DC

Daddy, Oscar and I had just started to gather our things to leave Fort DuPont Park. We frequented the park often to take in the sounds of the artists who performed in the Jazz in the Park venue. I really didn't care for the music, but Daddy said I should always try to experience new things; besides he was making me go.

I handed the picnic basket from our lunch to Oscar. He was my father's most trusted employee. Needless to say, Oscar was Daddy's best friend. He was also the deadliest, and you would never catch me or my father out anywhere without Oscar in tow. He was always sporting twin *Desert Eagles* on his hips and he wasn't afraid to make them clap. Oscar didn't look like he was a killer which pleased him because it always made it easy for his opponent to underestimate him.

"Oscar, why does Daddy make me come to this bamma Jazz stuff? I would rather be at a go-go. All my friends are partying with Chuck Brown and listening to Backyard. Why do I have to be the only one of my friends who has to suffer through this weekly visit to Jazz in the Park?"

"YaYa, one day you will have the pleasure of taking over "The Family Business" and you will have to entertain other types of people. My sweet niece, you will be a great leader of the DC streets, and you will have to know how to dance with the devil. You will have to be cultured in many things." Oscar said.

Oscar called anyone that wasn't a nigga, the devil. He also liked to call my father's ring of terror, drugs, pimpin', and violence, "The Family Business" which they had been telling me was my destiny since I was two. Just as I was handing Oscar the other end of the blanket we had used to sit in the cool grass, my father pulled up in his brand new armored Hummer. We started to pack up the truck when a frail woman with a teenage looking dude approached us.

Oscar – who trusted no one – instinctively reached for the heat on his hip, exposing the butt of the gun on his right side. After a second glance, I could see that the walking stick figure that was approaching us was once my mother, Christa. She was dirty and looked as though she hadn't had a bath in weeks. Her clothes were ratchet, and her hair was a shitty mess. She reached out for me, but Oscar grabbed Christa before she could touch me.

"Oscar, don't touch me!" she scowled.

Oscar released her, not because he was sure she was safe, but because he couldn't believe what he was seeing. My father couldn't believe his eyes either. He was seeing the mother of his daughter looking worse than he could have ever imagined. The dude who had walked up on us with Christa stepped up like he could protect her from anything that might pop off. He looked as though a bath tub hadn't seen him in quite some time and that he had missed one too many meals. There was something about him though that gave off that, "Don't fuck with me" vibe.

"Funny seeing you here! You were always so predictable." Christa said as she walked up on my father who was standing with a look of guilt in his eyes. "Darnell how about you and I talk for a while? Maybe we could try and get that old thing back." Christa cackled.

I couldn't believe what I was hearing coming from the mouth of the woman who once was my mother. She had the nerve to be trying to hit on my Dad as if he were going to jump at the chance to fuck her.

"Dee, I want you to meet someone. Neko, this is Dee and that lil' black bitch is your sister, YaSheema. She is the reason we have no home son. She is the reason we ain't got nothing. That lil' whore stole everything from me, including my man!" She screamed pointing at me. She was staring at me through drug-riddled eyes that were evil little slits.

Darnell had had enough. "Christa, if you don't leave YaYa out of this and tell me what it is you are doing here, I swear they are gonna' find your ass in the Potomac by morning!" He barked.

"I don't want shit from you or that tramp YaYa." She scowled. "Look, I have decided to get myself cleaned up. I need some help Dee. I am fucked up. I dunno' what else to do. I have nowhere to go." She sobbed.

"I'm no good to Neko like this. I can't help him until I can help myself." Her tears flowed freely. There was no doubt in my mind this was an award-winning performance. The young man with her, who eerily resembled me, rolled his familiar grey eyes.

"Look Christa, you and the boy just get in the truck because I ain't gonna' have you putting on a show for the whole damn city to see!" Darnell said.

Christa lifted her head and thanked my father for being so gracious. She tried to look as if she was wiping away tears. Then she looked at me and winked her eye. I knew right then Momma had some shit with her and I was determined to find out what the deal was.

"I see you moved out of the hood Dee." Christa said as we walked into our home on Dumbarton Street, in the heart of historical Georgetown, DC.

Georgetown is a beautiful area in upper Northwest Washington, DC. It used to be exclusively for colored folks back in the day and then white folks ran the blacks out during the 50's and 60's. Now it's nothing but uppity white folks living in their million-dollar homes. Black folks in this part of DC were far and few between.

"Yeah, Georgetown was a better area to raise YaYa in. She could go to a better school, but we didn't have to move out of the actual city. I like it. I can sleep better knowing YaYa is safe here." Darnell said.

My Dad and Christa were making small talk and I didn't want to hear my mother's fake shit anymore. "Christa why are you here?" I said with my hands on my perfectly rounded twenty-six year old hips. "You gotta' have a reason. You must want something." I stated.

Christa whirled around and stated boldly, "I am your mother and you will respect me little girl!"

"Mother? More like a fucking drug addict!" I shouted. "You haven't been a mother to me my whole life, so don't try to come in here with that shit now! And respect? Why should I respect a two-dollar whore?" I spat.

Christa lunged for me and slapped me across my face. I was stunned that the nasty bitch had touched me. Oscar moved in fast.

"That's enough Christa! I will not have you beating on one another in here!" Oscar barked as he carried me out of the room kicking and hollering.

"Imma' get you; you better believe this shit ain't over!" I screamed.

I could see Christa staring at me like she knew what I said was true. Her days were numbered. I had no love for the woman who gave me life. I had no respect for her. I vowed right then and there that she would never get another chance to make me feel like I was the cause of her misery. I saw Neko watching me as I was being carried away. I knew I should have protected him from the wrath of Christa. I was not going to let her fuck up his life anymore than she already had. I was fortunate enough to have my father in my life. God only knew what he had been through in his.

CHAPTER 4

The House
Georgia Avenue
NW Washington, DC

"**G**irl, I wanted to knock her on her ass!" I said into the receiver of the cordless phone that I had glued to my ear. I was talking to my best friend ShaniQua.

ShaniQua still lived in my old hood in Trinidad NE. That's where I was born and raised until my father decided we needed to be upgraded. ShaniQua and I had been best friends since we were babies. She was the sister of one of my father's lieutenants who was responsible for dropping off product and picking up money.

My father paid his people well, so ShaniQua was well off; but she wasn't doing it big like I was. In the eyes of the folks in the hood, ShaniQua was a ghetto princess and people respected her gangster. NiQue and I were thick as thieves, and everyone in the streets knew we were going to be running shit once our folks passed on the torch. NiQue was on the thicker side just like me. She had a creamy complexion. She was a "red bone" with a mean swag. NiQue knew the power of pussy and used it frequently to get what she wanted.

"NiQue, I almost crushed her in front of my dad. I know she is down there trying to con her way back into the house, but I got plans for that ass." I said.

Just as we started to speak on some nigga NiQue was craving to give the booty to, I heard a knock on my door.

"NiQue, someone is at my door. It's probably my dad and I rather you not hear him let me have it about this hoe."

"Aight girl, call me when you're done." NiQue laughed as she hung up.

I hit the end button on the phone just as my father entered the room. "YaYa, Christa will be staying here until she gets herself clean." He stated with authority. "I will not tolerate the bickering between the two of you while she and Neko are here." He continued.

I stood there in shock as my father told me my crack head mother would be staying in our home while she rehabbed.

"Daddy, why does she have to stay here? Can't she go to a shelter? They got plenty of shelters for crack head whores." I whined.

I knew I had crossed a line. My father looked at me like he never had before and I knew what was coming next was not going to be good.

"YaSheema, I don't know who you think you are talking to, but it certainly ain't me. Did you forget about who calls the shots around this muthafucka'?" He growled.

I must have looked as though I was in shock about the whole thing because my father's face softened. "YaYa, it is only gonna' be for a hot minute and then she and Neko are out. This is temporary, just so she won't be dragging that boy from place to place. I am ordering *Ledo's* for you and Neko. I thought it would be a good idea if you and Neko spent some time together, seeing that he is your brother and all."

With that my father turned and walked out of my room. I thought my father had lost his damn mind. He let this woman sucker him into letting her stay. I knew the real reason my father let her stay, he had a soft spot for charity case youths like Neko.

He grew up without a loving home, and he never wanted to see a youngin' down on their luck and fighting just to live day by day.

I took all of those things into consideration and thought about my, "not so little brother" who I would get a chance to know. Christa and I could squash our shit for a little while for his sake. I eased out of my room to see if Neko was adjusting to his new surroundings. He was in the guest room sketching a picture.

"Wassup wit' chu'?" I asked sitting Indian style on the floor next to him.

"Nothing, just sketching a picture of you." He said with an innocence I instantly fell in love with. He seemed like he was nothing like our mother.

I sat with Neko long into the evening. I guess being an only child made me long for companionship. I never really realized that I wanted a sibling. Neko had just finished his pizza as though it were his last meal. I watched him closely and studied him. He was surprisingly well mannered for someone with a devastating upbringing as I am sure he had.

"Neko, this is your room."

He looked around like he was in a fairytale. "This is my room?" His grey eyes, which resembled mine, showed their appreciation. Neko pulled the blankets off of the bed and laid them neatly on the floor. He then gathered a fluffy pillow and placed it on the floor with the blankets.

"What are you doing?" I asked, curious to know why he wanted to sleep on the floor instead of the bed.

He stopped dead in his tracks. "I guess I'm just used to sleeping on the floor. Creature of habit you know? I usually gotta' sleep on the floor where ever we end up; so it's no big deal. She says I am young and I can handle it. Plus, I don't wanna' sleep with her. She always makes noises in her sleep." He laughed.

I couldn't believe some of the stuff Neko and I talked about.

My brother was forced to take care of my mother's strung out ass! I couldn't tell who the parent was and who the off spring was. Based on the conversation we had, it seemed like he did more taking care of Christa than she did of taking care of him. Neko and I talked until he fell asleep. I stared at him and promised myself that I would take care of him. I made up my mind that Christa would pay dearly for whatever she had forced my brother to live through; because I was certain that he had endured a lot.

CHAPTER 5

The Awaking
National Harbor
Fort Washington, MD

Two months had gone by and Christa still wasn't straight. NiQue and I were out shopping at the mall. It was Friday; better yet, it was Memorial Day Weekend. Everyone knew the spot to be at was Anacostia Park for the three major summer holidays: Memorial Day, Fourth of July and Labor Day. The niggas would be out and you had to be fly to catch the bait.

"Girl, you think Tonio gonna be at the park?" NiQue asked with excitement while looking at a pair of sandals.

We were in Tyson's Corner where you had to go if you wanted that fly shit. We loved shopping at Tyson's Corner because it was in a predominately white area. There was nothing but rich white people there, and they stayed the fuck out of your way because you looked like you were up to no good if you were black. We used to love the attention we got when we would cop some of the most expensive shit and pay cash for it. Those dumb broads would be picking their faces up off the floor when we would hit up *Bloomies* (Bloomingdales).

"Girl, damn if I know. You know how these niggas be acting'.

He and Twan say one thing and mean another." I said, looking through a rack of blouses.

Twan and Tonio were twins who still believed in dressing identically. I thought the shit was just for show until I realized those bamma niggas were dressing alike all the time. They were twenty seven and I couldn't figure out why they were still dressing alike I wasn't feeling it. The twins hustled and lived around Lincoln Heights, one of the most notorious projects in DC.

Twan was the better looking twin, but he wasn't shit in the bedroom. He had a dick the size of a toddler's. He couldn't eat pussy and he would almost always bust a nut after three strokes – give or take a stroke. Shit, fucking him was so bad that I would just lay there and wonder how the hell I could let him slither his trifling ass on top of me, pump three times, and then roll over snoring like he just put in that work. That shit had gone on long enough!

"I hope Tonio bring his fine ass on girl. I want some of that!" NiQue said, winding her body like she was a stripper.

NiQue was sprung for Tonio. He only wanted to see her after dark and behind closed doors. She was so clueless it was almost comical. He just dicked her down and went on about his business. NiQue was convinced that they were in a relationship. My girl needed to open her eyes about that nigga instead of her legs. She got like that when she was dating someone new.

"Who cares about either one of those ratchet niggas? We are supposed to be trying to find some new goodies. I ain't wasting an outfit to be hanging around Twan. Girl, all the niggas that's going to be up at Ana with their bikes…I'm trying to go for a ride bitch, and it won't be on Twan's lil dick!"

We both cracked up laughing as we walked to the counter to pay for our items. We shopped for a few more hours before deciding to make our way back towards Georgetown. When we arrived home, Christa was milling around the family room and I was not particularly happy to see her tired ass.

"Is that all you do? Spend money? Wait and see…he will cut you off the way he cut me off." She mumbled; referring to the bags filled with all of the items I had just purchased. She was high as gas prices. I knew Christa was trying to cause a scene and I had been doing really well not falling for her shit.

"He will not cut me off." I simply stated. I wasn't trying to get into an argument with her. I knew she was looking for anything to use as ammo to have Daddy on her side so she could post up a little longer. "I am in no mood for your shit today lady, so I advise you to get out of our way."

NiQue and I tried to get around her and up the staircase. Christa stepped in my path and grabbed me by my arm with a force I never knew she could have in that frail ass frame of hers.

"Look here little girl, before all is said and done 'round here, I will have all that you took from me. You owe me and I will get everything due to me." She said coldly.

I dropped my bags on the parquet floor and stepped up to Christa. I used one hand to back her into a wall and I grabbed her around her throat with the other hand.

"Maybe you don't understand, this is my house bitch, and if you think you are going to be here much longer you got me fucked up!"

I was shaking Christa. She had long since let go of the hold she had on my arm. Instead she was gasping for air and clutching at my hand around her neck.

"I see through this bullshit you trying to pull. Daddy may not see, it but I see it. Fuck it, I'll kill you myself!"

I took my other hand and placed it alongside the one that was cutting off her air supply. Christa started to turn red and I wanted her dead. I wanted to watch her fall to the floor lifeless. Just as I thought about snapping her neck like a chicken, NiQue stepped in and grabbed me.

"Nooo…YaYa!" She cried. "Not here, not now, we got company."

I looked over my shoulder only to see my new-found brother, Neko, watching me throttle and shake his no-good-ass Momma like a dog in the street. I released my grip from her throat and wanted to say something to Neko. The words wouldn't formulate. He just stood there looking from me to Christa and back again.

"What cha' got in the bag for me?" He chimed in trying to break up the bad scene.

"I might have something in here for you." I said hinting at the bags I had dropped in the confusion. I gathered my belongings, and Neko and NiQue followed me up the stairs as if nothing had even happened.

"Awww, shit! YaYa your brother got it going on! Here try this." NiQue said to him handing him a black fitted cap that matched the jeans and *Jordan's* he was proudly sporting.

Neko looked happy and I was grateful that I had the chance to spend time with him. Just when I thought my day was going better, there was a knock on my bedroom door. I swung open the door to find Christa on the other side of it with her bags behind her.

"Neko, take off that silly shit and come on let's go!" She said like she was talking to a child instead of a grown man. Her words cut through me like a knife. *Where did she think she was going with my brother?*

"Christa, go ahead with all that. You know you ain't going anywhere and neither is he." I said pointing to Neko who stood off to the side looking for any reason to go with Christa.

"That's my son, not yours. Neko, I know you ain't really considering staying here with all I have done for you. Hell, I took care of you by myself all your life." Christa whimpered as she pushed her way into my room.

Neko just stood there off in the corner not wanting to be taken from his new home and his newly-acquired sister. He enjoyed the new life he had been given, and could not see going back to the way things were before they had found me and Daddy. Christa grabbed Neko and tried to exit my room. NiQue jumped up and blocked the doorway and I got a few things off my chest.

"I don't know what little games you think you are playing Christa, but I don't give a fuck if you leave; better yet, take this as a warning: get out of my house in the next twenty-four hours or you will live to regret it! As a matter of fact, you won't live to regret it!" I said cruelly. "Neko stays." I walked right past NiQue and flung the door open. "Neko, give me and Christa a moment to talk." I said while motioning for him to exit the room.

He smirked before picking up his newly-purchased clothes and shoes, and then headed out of the room. Christa stood dumb founded, like she couldn't believe her own flesh and blood could toss her out on the streets. She became enraged with the thought of being tossed out again, and like a wild animal, she lunged at me. I was caught off guard for a moment, not really recognizing what was about to go down, and NiQue quickly sprang into action for me. She grabbed Christa and the scuffle began.

"You little ghetto trash…get the fuck off of me!" Christa screamed. It was too late because NiQue had pinned Christa down to the floor and began wildly slapping her like she owed her money.

"You see bitch, you just brought your one way ticket out of here!" I said icily.

I sauntered across the room and reached into my night stand and pulled out my butterfly switchblade. Walking over to the woman who gave me life, I stooped down beside her and whispered the last thing she would ever hear.

"I'll see you in hell Christa!"

With one swift motion, I slid the knife from one side of her neck to the other with no remorse. Christa gargled and tried to stop the blood that was flowing from the open incision in her throat.

What Christa didn't know was that she had bred a killer. NiQue covered Christa's mouth to stop the sounds of her choking on her own blood. She finally stopped thrashing around and her grey eyes shut. She would never get another chance to hurt me or my brother again.

NiQue, being the ride or die bitch she was, dismounted Christa's lifeless body and left the room. She came back in seconds with an old blanket and a plastic table cloth we kept for picnics. We spread the plastic tablecloth on the floor and rolled Christa onto it. Luckily, years of drug abuse made it easy for us. She had done so many drugs she couldn't have weighed more than 90 pounds. After wrapping her up in the plastic and blanket, we moved her to the side. I went to the maid's closet and retrieved the mop and supplies to clean the wood floors.

I knew Daddy and Oscar were out, so getting out of the house with Christa's remains would be easy. Neko was safe because the housekeeper was on duty and I left her instructions to keep an eye on him. I gave her a "C" note and she went off to finish her duties. I didn't know how Neko might react if he came looking for me or Christa and neither of us were there. Even with him obviously having gone through a lot with Christa in his lifetime, I could tell that he still loved her.

NiQue pulled her Denali around to the back of the house. Together, she and I loaded Christa in the truck and headed in silence to Ana. Nightfall was approaching and we drove through the city of Downtown DC with Christa in the back of the truck.

"NiQue pull over right here," I instructed." I need to grab something."

I had a plan. I stepped out of the truck and surveyed my surroundings. After making sure no one was in the construction lot where I made NiQue stop, I ran over to a pile of concrete and began hauling blocks of cement to the truck. After four trips and several pieces of cement later, I got back in the truck and NiQue pulled off.

After several more minutes of driving, nightfall fell upon us as we pulled into Anacostia Park. The park was off limits after dark so we had to move fast. NiQue and I removed Christa's corpse and I tied thick plastic bags all around her body. Then I inserted the cement into the bags and we dumped my mother's body into the Potomac. NiQue never questioned any of the moves we made; she simply went with the flow. I got into the driver's side of NiQue's truck and we pulled away. As we exited the park and I looked down at my hands and noticed that they were covered in grime from the cement blocks.

"Dammit! I broke a nail fucking around with that bitch!" I said.

NiQue looked at me with a wide-eyed stare. She finally said something after what seemed like an eternity. "Where the fuck are you gonna' go and have that fixed?"

CHAPTER 6

The Shrimp Boat
Benning Road and East Capitol Street
NE Washington, DC

After NiQue and I returned to Georgetown, she decided she'd had enough excitement for the evening and she left to head towards her own home. I hadn't even remembered Neko was in the house until I heard him knock on my door. He entered the room looking a little frightened. Maybe he thought Christa would walk in at any moment and demand that he leave with her.

"Hey Shorty, wassup?" I said trying to make him relax a little. He found a clear spot on my bed and took a seat.

"Nothing. Where's Momma?" he asked. For the first time, it dawned on me that I hadn't really thought what my explanation was going to be about her whereabouts.

"Neko, she is gone and it is better that way anyway. You get to stay with me and Daddy." I saw his eyes perk up at that sound of that.

"Neko, she wanted me to take care of you. You will like it here with us."

I watched as Neko lay back on the bed like he was buying the whole story. I knew I would have a tougher time explaining what happened to Christa to my Dad, but that was something I would try and think about when the time came. The clock read midnight, and Neko was balled up in my bed. I couldn't sleep. Instead of the weed I had just smoked making me sleepy, it had me on edge and I needed to find something to do. I decided a game of pool would calm me. I left my room and ran straight into Daddy.

"Where's Christa?" he asked.

I motioned for him to join me downstairs. Once we were seated at the dining room table, I contemplated on how to tell him she was gone and wasn't gonna' come back. "Daddy, she's gone." I said trying to sound like I didn't know what had happened to her.

Daddy eyed me suspiciously. "Gone! She just left? I checked her room and all of her shit is still in there."

"She and I had a fight in front of Neko, and she said she was leaving with or without him." I started to sob hoping he wouldn't pry too much.

"YaYa, what is with all of the water works? You don't give a fuck 'bout her. When did you start caring about her leaving? For the past two months you tried to do everything in your power to get the bitch out!"

I knew my father could see right through my lies and I wanted to come clean. I started to crack my knuckles. That is what I do when I am nervous. Daddy picked up on that instantly.

"YaSheema, would you like to tell me what really happened that made Christa leave? I know there's no way she was just gonna' pick up and leave and not take anything with her." He said calmly.

I knew I had better tell him or continue to get drilled. "Daddy…" I started slowly. "I never meant for it to happen. It just did. Christa and I got into another argument and she tried to put her hands on me and I don't know what happened. I just reacted. I reached for my blade and I…" My voice cracked. I stopped to look up at my father who stood emotionless. I was hoping he wasn't gonna make me tell the whole story but the look in his eyes said he wanted details.

"I slit her throat and dumped her." I blurted out.

Daddy slid his chair out and walked to where I was sitting. He looked at me with so much love that it confused me. I had just confessed to killing my mother, and my father had the nerve to act as though I had just told him I had gotten accepted to Harvard.

"Sometimes we do things we don't wanna do and we have to live with it for the rest of our lives. Sometimes, we do things to protect the ones we love the most. Whatever the reason, never regret it. Regret will get you caught up. In time, you will learn how to handle shit like this. You will eventually learn how to turn your feelings off altogether. The best warriors were cold blooded. They made themselves numb to feelings and emotions."

I shuddered at the lesson my father was teaching me. Yeah, I had done some devious shit in my lifetime, but nothing could compare to what I had just done. Yet my father was sitting there nonchalantly; explaining that killing my mother was ok and that she was simply a casualty of war.

"I know I've done some shit that if the Feds knew about it, I would've been knocked a long time ago. This is just the beginning. You will end up taking my place YaYa, and there will be people who will try and stop you. You always have to think on your feet, and if it comes down to you or them, you better make sure it's the other nigga. Fuck everyone else because no one else cares about us. This family should always protect itself no matter who gets in the way. If we cannot hold strong as a family, any muthafucka' on the streets will succeed in taking us down.

You know I wondered if you would ever be ready to see what I am about and now I know it is time to get you ready to get this money out here. We will talk about all of this later." He said as he turned to leave the dining room. "Oh, and YaYa...you did take care of all of the particulars concerning Christa didn't you?" I looked at him confused. I wasn't sure what he was asking me.

"Has everything been disposed of?" He asked me as though he were inside my head. I nodded my head up and down. "Good. I take it Neko knows nothing of this?" He questioned. I finally found the courage to speak.

"Yes, I took care of letting him know Christa was gone and she wanted us to take care of him." I said.

"Good." That was all my father said as he left the room. I felt relieved that my father was in my corner about everything. I knew if Daddy could forgive and forget, so could God.

CHAPTER 7

Anacostia Park
SE Washington, D.C.

Three days later, NiQue and I were cruising through Anacostia Park. It was Memorial Day and Ana was on point. There were people cooking out and music was thumping from the cars that were riding the strip. We rode through the park twice before we found a place to park near where the rest of our folks were partying. We were not too far from the spot where only three nights before we had dumped Christa. I was on a mission to find someone that could help me relieve some of the sexual tension I had been feeling. We pulled in the spot next to Sheik's Chrysler 300 with the custom paint and deep dish rims. Sheik was definitely a catch, and his money was long.

NiQue and I stepped out of the truck looking like we were royalty and all eyes were on us. We commanded attention and we knew it. I pulled my shades down over my eyes, waiving at a few of the girls we came up with while I focused in on my prey. NiQue went off to be the social butterfly that she was known to be. I had one goal in mind, and that was posting up on Sheik.

Sheik was a chocolate drop sent from the heavens. He stood

6'2" and his body was rock hard. Just the way I liked it. He had long, thick locks that hung well past his shoulders. When he smiled, he displayed thirty-two white teeth. His demeanor was thug. He ate, slept, and breathed the streets. He was the one. I had to have him. He was absolutely delicious looking, dressed in a white tee and a pair of cargo shorts with fresh *Airforce Ones*. Nigga was fly by design and he knew it.

I sashayed over to where he and a few other niggas from around the way were engaged in a debate over who had the best track record with the ladies. They quieted the conversation once I spread my blanket out on the grass under the shade of one of the trees that lined the park. Once I knew all eyes were watching me, I bent over in my mini skirt just enough for them to see the one good thing my momma gave me. I sat the cooler down and stretched out on the blanket and acted as though I could care less that they were watching me. Actually, I didn't care if they did, just as long as the right person had his eyes on the prize.

Domo, a grimy, no money getting ass nigga was the first one to speak. "Wassup YaYa? Ma' you looking good over there. What you got in that cooler?"

Pulling my shades down to the tip of my nose and sucking my teeth. I uttered a tired "Wassup Domo, ain't nothing in there but some *Corona's*." That tired ass nigga was already getting on my nerves and he hadn't even said much yet. The entire time I was eyeing Sheik who simply glanced at me and went back to cooking the food he had on the grill. He acted as if I didn't turn him on and that pissed me off. I got up and sauntered over to where Sheik was manning the grill.

"Wha' chu' got going on over here?" I asked him seductively.

"Nuthin' Ma', just some burgers, chicken, some ribs and some other stuff. You know how we do. Why? What you want?" He asked.

I took off my shades and swung my freshly done wrap. I looked him up and down and simply said, "You."

"Go ahead Shorty," He laughed. "I ain't got time to play games with you."

I was angry that he had shot me down, but I couldn't front, he turned me on . No man had ever turned me down, and I wasn't about to start letting the niggas out here carry me. "I am a grown ass woman and I damn sure don't play kiddy ass games. You just let the best thing to ever grace your presence get away." With that, I dipped off before he could see I was angry about him shooting me down in front of his homeboys. I heard his boys telling him he was stupid, and calling him a "lame" for not trying to get up with me. Domo's nasty ass even went as far as to say he thought Sheik was a faggot for turning me down.

I walked through the park to see if I could catch up with NiQue. I was nursing a slightly bruised ego and needed my friend for backup. Hearing a familiar voice, I turned to see who was trying to get my attention. It was a dude from Saratoga named Papi, and he was waving for me to come to him. Papi wasn't doing as much as he thought he was, but he was making moves. Originally from Baltimore, he was moving weight between Up top and NW Baltimore, including a few places in between. He was known to be a lover, and the chicks dug him because he spent that cash. The bitches liked him because he was a trick. I had heard he had a few folks under his belt and was a shiesty ass nigga.

"What it do Papi?" I asked.

Papi wasn't all that easy on the eyes, but he could be good for a few dollars in the pockets. Being part Cuban and part Nigerian, I had to admit, he had a lot of natural born swagger. As I walked towards him, Papi licked his thick lips and began laying his game down. He looked like he was hungry, and I was going to be his last meal before going to prison.

"Why are you out here alone?" He asked, trying to see if I had come with someone or not.

"I'm not alone. My girl NiQue is out here somewhere and the rest of my folks are over there on the grill." I said pointing in the direction of Sheik and Domo. Papi looked like he had seen a ghost when he locked eyes with Sheik. He quickly regained his composure and tried rapping me up again.

"Oh, so you over there with your man and his lame ass friends huh?" He said trying to make himself feel like a hood star. I figured if Sheik didn't want me I would make him feel like he was missing something special.

"Naw, those are just my friends." I said nonchalantly.

"Well YaYa, you are here with me now." He pulled me into him like we were lovers.

I had gotten so wrapped up in making a public scene with Papi that I had totally forgotten about NiQue. He had me sitting under a shelter with him, his boys, and some bitches who were giving me the evil eye.

"Papi, I really have to go and find my friend. She is probably looking for me." I said as I tried to leave.

He wasn't happy about me trying to leave the little party he and his boys were throwing; but the truth of the matter was that I hadn't seen NiQue in over forty-five minutes. Our rule was if we come together, we leave together, unless we mutually agree to split up.

"I'll see you later tonight. Make sure you make yourself available. Don't keep a nigga waiting!" He said.

He walked over to his car and started blasting "Hood Star" by Coogi Ty. The females who were in our immediate vicinity started to party. One girl dropped low to the ground in front of Papi and was simulating riding dick. He didn't even look back to make sure I was gone before he had the trick bent over the hood of his car grinding his dick on her to the beat of the music. I was glad they were helping me make it easy to get away from him.

I headed towards the spot where everyone else was still drunk and partying. My blanket and cooler were just where I left them and Sheik and Domo were still listening to music and talking shit. I re-joined the group and their conversation. Sheik was the first to ask me about Papi.

"Aye Yo YaYa, wassup with that fake ass nigga you were with? That nigga be out here on the streets faking. You need to leave his dirty ass alone. That nigga will rob your young ass blind and we know Pops will light into you." They all laughed.

"I can handle myself. I got this." I went to my cooler and pulled out two fifths of *Patron Anejo*.

"Shots anyone?" I asked the whole group. Half of those thirsty niggas was with it. We all set up for shots. Domo eyed the *Patron*. "I thought you didn't have anything in there but beer. I knew your ass was lying." Domo said holding his cup up. Ten or so shots later I was busted. Sheik and company looked as if they were done too.

NiQue finally showed up as I was getting into Sheik's grill about not wanting to taste me. Sheik was dusted, but he was still holding strong about not fucking with me and I was tired of trying. As she walked towards me, there was a glow about NiQue, and she wasn't alone. She had Shawnna and Twan with her. Looking at her, I immediately know why I hadn't seen her in over an hour. She had probably rolled out to meet up with Twan so he could get his rocks off before moving on to his next pussy mission.

Shawnna was the chick that Sheik was dealing with, and at the sight of her I wasn't in a partying mood anymore. The bitch was my competition and I wasn't in the mood to act like I wasn't aware of that fact. Just as I was thinking of how to get out of their presence, NiQue announced that we needed to get moving to make sure we hit all of the Memorial Day party spots. I was glad my friend was ready to roll because I sure wasn't in the mood to watch Sheik and

Shawnna engage in their love affair. Call me naïve, but I always got what I wanted. Even if that meant I had to act childish or whorish to get it and I was going to get a piece of Sheik.

CHAPTER 8

Ben's Chili Bowl
U Street
NW Washington, DC

Just as I had packed up my things into the back of NiQue's truck my cell phone started ringing. The number was one I didn't recognize. Against my better judgment I answered it. On the other end of the line was Papi. For the life of me I didn't remember giving him my number.

"Wassup Ma?" He slurred. I knew he was just as dusted as I was.

"Wassup Papi?" I responded, not really wanting to talk to him.

"I was trying to see what was up with you for the rest of the night. Maybe we can go out and maybe in the morning we can go shopping or something.

I perked up at the sound of shopping. It wasn't like I was hurting for cash, I just wasn't turning down spending that nigga's money. Papi snapped me out of my thoughts of those new *Baby Phat* sandals I wanted.

"Ma, where did you say you were again?"

"I am headed towards NiQue's. How did you get my number? I don't remember giving it to you." I asked.

"Bet, I will meet you over there." He said and hung up the phone before I could even tell him I had other plans. An hour went by before I heard a loud horn honking in front of NiQue's house. I had just adjusted my make-up and ran my fingers through my hair. I peered out of the master bedroom window.

"Shit. I forgot that nigga said he was gonna slide through. NiQue, who had just stepped out of her bathroom with a towel wrapped tightly around her body, looked confused.

"Who is that outside leaning on their horn like that? Where are you going? I thought we were going to the club."

"Girl we are! That's Papi. He decided to come through here. I told him I was headed this way and he must have just dropped pass."

I gave her the "trust me we are going out" spiel and headed towards the door to handle that nigga.

When I got to his car I could tell he had sobered up a bit. He had changed his clothes and looked better in the cover of night. He was tall and muscular which made him fuckable. He had the body of a God! The way he leaned on the side of his car watching me made my panties moist. His presence demanded respect. Money, power, and respect; that's what it took to make me weak. I stepped into an embrace that Papi offered.

"Ma, you looking good. Aye let's bounce." It dawned on me that he wasn't asking.

I figured I better speak up and let it be known I had other plans. "Papi, I was on my way out to the club with NiQue. You never gave me time to hip you to that."

"The club?" He laughed. "YaYa, you got me fucked up if you are thinking about going to the club when I drove all the way over here." He growled.

My face began to get warm and I could feel my temper rising. "Yeah, you never said we were going anywhere and I made plans with my girl." I tried to explain rationally.

"Your girl probably ain't even ready to roll yet. Ya'll always take forever getting ready." His tone changed and he settled down a bit. He was right though, NiQue was barely out of the shower. An hour wouldn't hurt.

"She will be ready to go in an hour so that is all you're going to get." I said turning to head back in the house. I knew I had better think of something to tell NiQue, and I'd better think fast. After a good cursing out, I was in Papi's SC 430 Lexus heading towards God knows where with him. We hit up Ben's Chili Bowl and Papi started making his way to I-495.

"You know it's been over an hour. I really need to be getting back to NiQue."

"I already told her she can go out without you." He said never taking his eyes off of the road. I looked at Papi confused. How had he gotten NiQue's number to tell her that? I looked at him full of curiosity. That was the second time tonight he had gotten info on me that I hadn't given.

"How did you get her number? As a matter of fact, how did you get mine?" I questioned.

Papi kept his eyes on the road and tried to act as though he hadn't heard my questions. I couldn't believe he was just going to ignore anything I said that he didn't want to hear. We pulled into a driveway to a moderate home close to the outskirts of Baltimore. From the outside the house was average, but once inside I was amazed at how beautiful the house was. He had very good taste.

"Go and check out the rest of the house. Wha' cha' sippin' on?" Papi seemed anxious for me to look around. Nigga wanted me to be impressed.

"I started with *Patron*, I might as well finish the night off with it too." I responded.

I had already scoped out the well-stocked bar. I peered beyond the entertainment area of his home and marveled by the choice of colors and the décor. It wasn't typical of a street nigga to have that much style. His house was laced with flat screen TV's, and there were speakers built into each wall. The kitchen was state of the art and the entire place just screamed, "You can have the panties." I silently wondered how many women had come there and dropped their drawls for him already.

I turned my attention to a painting of a woman on Papi's wall that hung over the cream-colored Italian leather furniture. The woman was in her mid to late forties. She wasn't all that pretty, but she had a glow about her that oozed sexiness. I figured the painting was his sister or another relative because she shared similar features as he did.

"Oh, you like that portrait? That's my mother." He said handing me a shot glass. He sat the bottle of *Patron* on the table and patted the seat next to him. I sat my *Coach* bag on the table and grabbed the bottle. After a few glasses, we were pretty loaded and enjoying each other's company when Papi started firing away with questions.

"YaYa, what do you know about this life? Really, do you know what kind of life you live? Power demands power; and I need power by my side. You gonna ride with me?"

I couldn't believe he was really trying to get up with me like that. We barely knew each other on that level and he had a bad rep for being a trick. "Papi you ain't trying to fuck with me for real. I know what kind of shit you're into." I said.

"You don't know what I'm into. I'm a business man; just like your father."

Somehow Papi mentioning my father didn't sit right with me. I know my father has some serious street credibility, but why did he bring him up right then?

"Papi, I have some stuff going on with my parents and I am trying to make my own way out here. I need to get my own life right first." I lied. He didn't need to know I could run circles around him in the streets. Daddy always saw to it that no one knew I was heavily involved in his organization. I liked to keep all of my options open, and Papi and I being together was not in my game plan. I had other missions to accomplish. I was buying time until I got with Sheik. That's where I wanted to be. Thoughts of Sheik started racing through my mind and for just a moment, I pretended Papi was Sheik.

I moved closer to on the couch towards him. I wanted him to want me. I figured why not get some satisfaction while waiting for the real thing. Papi got the clue and started pinching my nipples through the fabric of my sheer shirt. His touch was just right. I felt the nectar between my legs and I knew I needed it more than Papi even knew.

"Stand up." Papi said with authority. "Let me look at what's going to be mine."

I smirked at him and stood up. I lifted my shirt over my head and slid out of my skirt. I stood in front of Papi in a red bra and thong set and a pair of stilettos from *Steve Madden*. I knew I looked like candy. My chocolate skin glowed, and I knew exactly what looked good on it. I turned around and bent over so he could see my full round ass. I made it clap for him and ran my finger over my pussy. I was putting on a hell of a show. I knew my audience was pleased.

Sliding off my thong, I pushed Papi back on the couch. I straddled his muscular legs and started to grind on his hard dick that was struggling to get free from his pants. I was going to show him a good time; not because I wanted to fuck with Papi like that, but because I wanted to be wanted. Papi unfastened my bra and suckled on my nipples until they were hard and begging to be bit. As if he knew the urgent need of my body, he gently bit and tugged on my nipples sending me into a sexual frenzy. I started to grind my pussy harder on his manhood and came on his pants.

I dismounted Papi and he stood and led me up the stairs to the master bedroom. Dropping his pants with a quickness, he exposed all ten inches of himself. Then he laid me down on the bed and made my center his dinner. He kissed and sucked my pussy until I was on the brink of orgasm. Papi was doing shit to me I hadn't had in a while, and my body was thankful for the gift. I started to grind my pussy on his lips and he grabbed my ass encouraging me to cum.

"Dat's right Ma.'" he said. His accent was more defined than before. "Cum for me." He whispered between muffled kisses.

Not being able to control the urge anymore, I came again. I felt the need to return the favor and sat on the edge of the bed and took all ten inches of Papi into my mouth while he stood towering over me. He rolled his head back as I sucked on his candy until I felt his legs begin to shake. I took in his dick one last time as far as it would go and let him fall from my lips. I climbed up onto the bed and got on all fours. I arched my back and wiggled my ass. Papi pulled me to him by my waist and entered me. His dick was so thick and juicy. He thrust into my wet pussy causing me to shudder. He smacked my ass and I winched from the pain that was bringing me so much pleasure. Papi pulled out of my dripping pussy and lay on his back.

"Sit on the thrown!" He commanded.

I obliged. I sat on his dick, bouncing up and down, riding him like a pro. Papi slammed me down on his dick making me take all of him into my walls.

"Sssssss…YaYa this pussy is mine!" He yelled. I tightened my walls around his thick dick and we came together.

We lay there in his bed for an entire day. Fucking and sleeping. Every time I thought about leaving, Papi beckoned me back with his incredible sex.

Chapter 9

Over the span of several months, my father put me in position to meet his supplier. I had just turned twenty-seven, and DC wasn't ready for me. Daddy's supplier was a greasy Columbian named Caesar. Caesar made it well known that he was not too fond of having to deal with someone other than Daddy, and definitely not eager to deal with a bitch. Daddy's reputation of making bread and the fact that he wasn't afraid to bust his guns made Caesar humble himself in Daddy's presence. After several meetings, several threats, and long negotiations, Caesar agreed to conduct all business transactions through me. He wasn't going to mess up his lavish lifestyle just because he didn't think a woman could hold it down in the streets.

Up until today, I had been traveling with Daddy and Oscar to complete transactions. Darnell Clayton was getting money and he was making sure that everyone he was affiliated with knew that I would be taking the reins. Today was different though. I would be handling a minor change in business with Caesar alone.

I slid into a black silk camisole and a cream-colored suit that looked like *Christian Dior* made it just for me. The flared leg pants suit accompanied by a pair of stilettos made my ass sit up like an apple. I grabbed my purse and briefcase and made a bee-line for the door. I didn't want to be late. It was time to shit or get off the pot.

I pulled my shades down over my eyes and pulled my chrome-colored Cadillac STS out of the driveway. As I made my way onto Wisconsin Ave, I checked my rearview mirror for Oscar. He was right there two cars behind me. Daddy said for our safety, I was to ride in my own car and Oscar was to follow me in his own ride. So if something popped off, help was nearby.

I changed the music on my *Ipod*. 'Shawty' by Plies filled the *Bose* speakers. I instantly thought of Sheik. He was my goal, and I hadn't invested any time on my personal mission. Never mind the fact that Papi was fucking me proper on a regular basis. He was constantly trying to make me wifey. That shit was growing old and at this point I am bored with it. He had been flaunting me around and spent bread, but he was too eager to make "us" into something I had no interest in. He wanted me to introduce him to my father. That shit was out of the question. I was a grown woman, but I didn't want my father to even think I was involved with anyone. Daddy's motto was, "Always money over hoes" and Papi was a hoe.

Papi had been asking about Daddy a lot and it was definitely uncomfortable. I couldn't figure out his fascination with my father. I sparked the El I had rolled before leaving the house and my mind drifted back to the task at hand. I was nervous about going to see Caesar. He didn't like me and the feeling was mutual. I knew he was only tolerating me because of my father.

What sealed the deal was my father threatening to take his money elsewhere if Caesar would not accept Daddy's demands. At the rate my father was moving bricks through the DMV (DC, MD, and VA), Caesar knew better than to be too defiant. By the time I stepped into the organization full time, Daddy's street team was moving twenty bricks a week. Caesar would have been a fool to fuck up the twenty-two grand per brick, per week, that he was seeing.

I finished the El and aired out the car as I drove across the Woodrow Wilson Bridge. I had finally made it to Caesar's lavish home in Fairfax, Virginia. I dabbed my wrists with my signature scent of *Meditation* and exited the car. Oscar joined me by my side and buzzed the intercom.

"Hola." a woman said through the speaker.

"I have an appointment with Caesar. This is Ms. Clayton." I stated.

A few moments later, we're greeted by a sexy Latina who was wearing the hell out of a *Dolce and Gabbana* contour A-line suit. She ushered us inside and led us to Caesar's office where he was blowing smoke rings from his foul smelling Cuban cigar.

"Good day Ms. Clayton. How are we today?" He said as we took a seat around a marble table with wing back chairs that looked like they cost a small fortune. I hated the way he said my name. He nodded towards Oscar to acknowledge his presence.

"Hello Caesar. We are well." I responded; not interested in the small talk. I was here to conduct business and that was all I planned to do.

"Can I interest you in a drink?" He offered. I declined his offer and tried to keep the meeting moving in the right direction.

"Caesar, my father has been buying product from you at twenty-two per kilo, and we have been moving twenty bricks a week, and we often run low, or out altogether at times. We now see it is time to increase our supply. We are asking to decrease the sales price from twenty-two to twenty per kilo.

Caesar looked at me amused. "Lil' girl, chu' are bold. Chu' have balls bigger than your father. Do you really think you can waltz in here and make requests such as these?" He laughed and as he did... my demeanor remained the same.

"I am prepared to take my business elsewhere if you are unwilling or unable to accommodate. I stated sternly.

"Why should I trust that chu' will make good on your purchases?" Caesar inquired.

"You just have to trust me and my abilities to make it happen." I said with my eyes locked on Caesar.

"Oscar, can you excuse us for a moment?" I asked, never letting my gaze leave my intended target. Oscar pushed his chair from the table and glared at me. I could tell his eyes were questioning my motives for asking him to wait outside the office. Once Oscar left the office, I focused in on Caesar's greasy ass. I stood up and moved towards his seat. Caesar watched my every move. I took off the jacket to my suit and draped it on the chair that was closest to him.

"Look Caesar, we need to be able to trust one another." I said seductively.

Caesar licked his lips, and motioned for me to move closer to him. For him to hate doing business with females, it sure seemed like he had no qualms with mixing our business with pleasure. This was fine by me as long as it sealed the deal. I slid off my pants and Caesar pushed me to my knees. Unzipping his pants, I released what had to be the tiniest dick I had ever laid my eyes on. I put the head of his dick in mouth and began sucking him off to let him know that working with me would bring him more gratification than just money.

He began to thrust himself into my mouth. I met him at each stroke and knew he was enjoying his bonus for working with me. Caesar grabbed the back of my head and he started to moan. I picked up my speed to hurry him along. He was thrusting in and out of my mouth with fast strokes and I knew he was ready to explode. I pulled him out of my mouth.

"Do we have a deal?" I asked looking him dead in his eyes.

"Chu' drive a hard bargain Ms. Clayton. We have a deal." He said as he grabbed the back of my head and I took him back into my mouth. He stroked my mouth several more times before delivering his babies. Once he was finished, I rose to my feet and pulled my clothes on. I opened my briefcase and handed him my new purchase orders and his money to provide my product. He informed me of where our next pick up would be and I exited his office as if nothing had ever happened. Oscar was right outside the door when I exited and he gave me a concerned look.

"Oscar the deal is done. I have the instructions for our next pick up and a new buy price." I said casually.

"YaYa, how were you able to do that? He was clearly puzzled as to how I was able to talk Caesar down.

"I simply let him know working with me, instead of against me, was the best and only option for him." I said coldly.

Oscar asked no more questions as we left the house accompanied by the same Latina chick we had seen earlier. He watched me closely. He knew I was definitely a product of my father's seed. Oscar and I went to our respective cars and drove off together much richer than we had come. I picked up my cell phone and dialed my father. I let him know the deal was done and that I had the new orders in motion. I knew just what I needed as a reward for handling my first business transaction and I knew just who could give it to me.

I pulled my Caddy onto I-495 North and headed towards Baltimore. I knew Papi would quiet the fire I had growing down below. You see, money turned me into an animal. I lusted after money, and just knowing I was about to be ten times richer than I already was got me all the way to B-more on a mission to twerk with Papi's freaked-out ass.

CHAPTER 10

The Tradewinds Night Club
Old Branch Avenue
Temple Hills, MD

I made it around the Beltway in record time. I was hoping Papi was either home or on his way home when I got there. Once I pulled up in the driveway, I noticed he must have had company because an unfamiliar car was parked in the driveway along with his. High and horny, I knew that whoever was there was gonna have to hurry their business along and keep it moving. I walked up the small cobblestone walkway and tried the knob. I found it unlocked and let myself in. Walking into the living room, I found Papi deeply engaged in a conversation with two big Spanish dudes who looked like they were real unhappy about being there. Once they spotted me the conversation ceased.

"I didn't mean to interrupt, I will let myself out." I said feeling awkward for walking in unannounced. I quickly started to make my exit.

Papi hopped up out of the seat he was in. "No, we were just finishing up." He said looking around nervously. There was definitely something wrong with the meeting they were having. Papi's face was covered in beads of perspiration, and his company looked as though they had murder on their minds.

"Si, Finito. Recordar lo que dije. Tener mi dinero o vamos a cortar tus bolas y a alimentarlas a tu novia hermosa después de que nosotros violación múltiple ella." Said the bigger of the two men.

A look of sheer horror danced across Papi's face. The men turned to leave. One of them stopped short of leaving and turned to grab my hand. "Adios, mi amiga." He kissed my hand and strolled out of the door.

"What was all that about?" I questioned.

Too bad I failed all those years of Spanish in high school. It may have come in handy today. Whatever they had said to Papi wasn't good because he was standing stark still and unresponsive to my question.

"Nothing baby, just a little business I had to handle. That's all." He said snapping out of his trance.

"It looked like they wanted to handle you." I said starting to regret coming all the way out to his place. Those two made the hair on the back of my neck stand up.

"Look YaYa, that was a stressful meeting and I don't want to go into it. What are you doing over here anyway?" He quizzed.

"I looked at his full lips and remembered what I had come there for. "I came to celebrate." I said seductively.

"What are you so happy about Ma?"

"Let's just say I had a very productive day." I said walking towards the stereo that was playing "Lollipop" by Lil' Wayne. I closed my eyes and started swaying my hips to the beat. Papi didn't look too concerned about his meeting anymore.

"I like the way you moving those hips Ma." Papi said watching me like a predator stalking his prey. I started stripping out of my suit for the second time today and let it hit the floor, exposing myself to him.

"Mami when are you gonna be mine?" Papi shot the question at me as I rode the rhythm of the music. I turned around so that my back was to him and made my ass clap. I could see approval on his face but that did not stop him from asking more questions.

"Why do you keep avoiding the question YaYa? You know how many bitches want to be in your position?"

"Do you know how many niggas want to be in yours?" I shot back. It never failed. Every time I went to Papi for sexual gratification, he wanted to make it into some relationship shit. I was not interested and the argument was getting old. Why couldn't he just fuck me and let that be enough? I thought females were the thirsty ones.

"Why can't we just be what we are right now? Why do we have to be with one another to enjoy each other?" I whined. I hoped that by whining he would get fed up and just lay the pipe and we could avoid all of the relationship business he kept pressing me about.

Papi stood up and walked over to me and grabbed me by my waist. His muscular hands made my body feel like it was aflame with desire. Papi laid me down on the leather couch on my stomach and began kissing my shoulders and made a path of warm kisses down to the small of my back and down my apple. He turned me over on my back and began rubbing his fingers over my womanhood. My breathing quickened and Papi knew it was time to deliver the goods. He stood over me and unfastened his jeans and in one motion, stooped down and entered me forcefully.

I loved when he made angry love to me. He used all of his might to prove that he was the best lover for me. Papi groaned in ecstasy as he plunged deeper into my sugary walls. I held on to him as if my life depended on him fucking me. I could feel his body tense up and I knew he was nearing the end of his supposed punishment.

"YaYa, sssssss... I'm about to cum!" He roared.

Papi exploded inside of me and lay there panting on top of

me. I hated when he came inside me. I rolled him off of me and headed towards the bathroom on the upper level of the house. I had only been upstairs for a few minutes before I heard Papi talking on the phone. I crept back into the hallway and leaned over the banister on the upper level of the house.

"Juan, just give me some time chico. I am working on something right now with the biggest connect in the city to get your money situated." I heard Papi say.

"I am bangin' this bitch and her father got shit locked in the DMV. I am sure things are about to jump off. I just need a few more weeks before I can seal the deal."

I backed into the master bedroom from which I had come and sat on the edge of the bed bewildered. I couldn't believe what I had just heard. Not only was Papi telling lies to people about us, but he was using my father's reputation to handle business. I had had enough of Papi and I knew that day would be the last time he would touch me. I quickly showered and pulled on a pair of Papi's sweatpants and a plain white t-shirt. I had left a pair of *Nike's* in Papi's closet the last time I had stayed the night with him.

Descending the stairway, I grabbed the rest of my belongings from where I had stripped out of them. I knew Papi and I had nothing to talk about anymore, and I wanted to make my exit quick without letting him know I had overheard his conversation. Papi was still on the phone when I picked up my purse and shades and he gave me a look of discontent about me leaving.

I didn't even speak. I couldn't speak. I was so pissed about him using me. I vowed that he and I would tango again, and I would buy my time until I could figure out how to punk the nigga for telling lies. I headed out the door, not wanting to engage in anymore of his bullshit.

CHAPTER 11

NiQue and I had made plans to meet in Old Town for a day at the spa. I had to fill her in on the details of Papi's betrayal.

"YaYa, I could have told you that nigga was up to no good. That nigga ain't interested in settling down with no bitch. He is all about getting money any way he knows how."

My mind drifted back to what Sheik had said to me about Papi being a sheisty ass nigga. I was enjoying the full body massage I was receiving, and NiQue was having the same done to her. In between exhaling, we continued to talk.

"I didn't have any intentions on dealing with him like that anyway. I was just getting my back blown out. I never wanted to fuck with this greasy nigga." I said while Becky, the masseuse, was kneading my lower back.

"This nigga was trying to play me!" I said.

"So, what are you going to do about it?" NiQue questioned.

"I think I am going to just leave him the fuck alone! I have business I have to handle for Daddy and I cannot let whatever Papi is cooking up get in my way."

I couldn't let Papi's deceit cloud my mind and sidetrack my business. I had to oversee my first transaction and nothing was going to get in my way. NiQue and I finished our spa treatment and headed back into the city. I hadn't really spent any time with Neko and I thought a movie would be a good idea. Will Smith had a new flick out, and I had heard it was better than the critics thought it would be. NiQue declined my invitation to join us and I dropped her at her place. I drove through the streets of DC wondering what kind of shit Papi was into and I couldn't shake the fact that the nigga was doing nothing more than using me to get to my Dad.

Papi had called several times since I left his house, and I wasn't interested in listening to whatever story he had for me. I switched the power off on my personal cell and started making phone calls on my business cell to a few of my lieutenants on the Southside. Corrine, a dyke broad I had ties to, was one of my best lieus. If you didn't know she was a woman, you would have never known. Corrine was 6'3" with long plaits that hung down her back. She kept herself rockin' fresh *Shooters* tees and she always had every custom tennis shoe available. She was notorious for keeping her foot soldiers in line, and if they ever fell out of line there would be blood spilled on the streets. I called Corrine to see if she had some ends for me to pick up.

"Yo, Corrine…what's up babes'?" I said.

"Wassup YaYa? You coming through here? I got them thangs ready for you. Oh, and I need to holla about making another move because this shit is selling out faster than I can move it."

"I got ya' baby. I should be through there in an hour or so and we can talk then." I said. I knew what was coming next because it always did when I spoke to Corrine.

"YaYa, when you gonna stop faking shawty and come to the other side. You went for a test ride and ain't never come back to claim the goods."

"Corrine, I keep telling you that I don't even swing like that. You know I want dick and unless you got one you were born with… then there ain't nothing you can do for me."

"Yeah aight, shawty. You gave it to me once; you'll give it to me again." She laughed.

"Yeah, we'll see. Oh, and Corrine…fuck you." I laughed as I hung up.

I had given Corrine some pussy a while back and since then, she wouldn't give up on trying to get it again. I knew that that lifestyle wasn't for me. I made my way from Trinidad to the Southside listening to Lil' Wayne and T-Pain. It seems that if you didn't have Weezy on your track, you weren't doing anything major. All the while during the drive I thought about Papi and how he was trying to use my Daddy to prosper. I knew something wasn't right and I was feeling like he was trying to set me up. I shook off the bad vibes and decided that I wanted to stop off at Henry's Soul Food Café and grab some real southern food.

I pulled up to the restaurant and instantly noticed Sheik's car parked out front. Looking in the rearview mirror, I touched up my *MAC* lip gloss and strolled inside. As soon as I walked in, I spotted him. He was sitting near the window by himself.

"Hi Sheik. How are you?"

"Wassup YaYa?" He asked while giving me the once over.

"I am good. I have been working trying to make a dollar out of fifteen cent." I responded.

He couldn't keep his milk chocolate eyes off of me. I was trying to play it cool because he had already proven he wasn't the ego trip type.

"May I join you?" I asked. It was more like me telling him I was going to sit there than me asking.

I sat my purse on the table and removed my glasses from my

face to expose my signature grey eyes. The waitress made her way to our table and took my order of baked turkey wings smothered in gravy, with mashed potatoes and collard greens. Sheik turned his attention back to me. "Where you gonna put all that? Why don't you go home and cook that kind of stuff. Or in your case, have the maid or the chef get that popping for you?"

"So glad you think it is that easy playboy. I work and I have no time to cook for myself, and the maid is a twenty-three-year-old chica who never fixed a turkey wing in her life. She damn sure doesn't know anything about collard greens. She's too busy running behind my father!" I retorted.

"Damn Ma', don't take my head off and you call what you are doing working huh? I hear your father got you handling that work. Are you still fucking with that cat Papi?" He asked.

I had been wondering if he was going to make the conversation personal at some point, or if he was going to brush me off as he usually did when we were in passing.

"For your information…yes, I am handling business for my father; and no, I am not dealing with Papi. Are you still dealing with Shawnna?" I asked trying to throw shade and pry for more information on his relationship status.

"Naw, she and I stopped messing with each other a little while back. She didn't wanna hold a nigga down. For real out here in these streets that's what a nigga needs; a shawty that will be there no matter what. Even though we may not be living right by society's standards, we are doing what we have to do to survive. I was willing to take care of her and give her all the fly shit she wanted, but she wanted me to leave the game. I am going to leave this shit alone real soon; but once I do, I have to make sure I never have to come back to the game. I got plans on making it big outside of the hustle. What about you YaYa? What are you gonna do with yourself? Shit, you shouldn't even be in this game your damn self."

That was the first time Sheik showed any interest in me and I didn't want him to lose focus.

"Well, I have been thinking about opening a clothing store or something like that. You know something that NiQue and I could do together. Maybe move to some place sunny. Maybe have some kids, do the family thing." I said not really meaning half of it, but it sure sounded good.

Sheik perked up like he believed the bull I was spitting.

"That sounds like a plan YaYa. You can't live off this dirty money forever. Your Dad was able to make it as long as he has because he is smart and has his hands in other ventures too. I respect him for his hustle."

The waitress returned with our food and we chatted for what seemed like hours. I never knew Sheik was so smart. I knew he was street savvy, but I didn't know he was so intelligent in other arenas. I looked down at the time and realized that I had Corrine's pickup and I also wanted to take Neko out. I laid a hundred dollar bill on the table and told Sheik he would have to forgive me for being rude, but I had business to tend to. I let him know dinner was on me and wrote my number on one of the napkins and left the café before he could even say anything.

I had been in there too long with money waiting to be collected. I hopped in my Caddy and pushed over to the Southside. Fortunately for me, Corrine's house wasn't too far from the café. I pulled up in the Villages of the Parklands in front of one of the units. Looking at the particular neighborhood during the day, you would never know it was one of the worst places to live in DC. The place housed mostly hustlers and drug abusers. All of whom were my clients in one way, form, or fashion.

Walking up to the front door of where Corrine had set up camp, I could here babies crying and smell the scent of some hydro in the air. I walked up the flight of stairs and instantly reached in my purse for my heat. I knocked on Corrine's door and I heard her say, "come in." I twisted the knob and Corrine looked like she was entertaining a few guests and not in the traditional manner. She was seated on the couch, and two girls were lying on the floor in front of her having sex. They didn't even bother to stop once they knew I was in the room.

Corrine had a look of satisfaction on her face when she saw the bewildered look on mine. I was watching the floor show, and I felt my pussy start to tingle. I knew I had better get what I came for and leave before I became a willing participant. I have always been a sucker for good head. I tore my eyes away from the show and focused on Corrine on the couch.

"The next time I am here to make a pick up can you make sure I don't have to walk into this gay shit." I boomed.

"YaYa, I don't even know why you are tripping. Besides you said an hour and it has been three since I spoke to you last. Was I supposed to keep them waiting?" She laughed pointing at the two broads who still hadn't come up for air.

Corrine rose off of the couch and motioned for me to follow her to the back. With every step I took to follow her, I could feel the tingle getting stronger. We entered what looked to be her office which housed a 37 inch flat screen TV, and a top of the line *Dell* computer system complete with scanner and printers. She sat down behind her cherry wood desk and pulled a briefcase from underneath it. She unfastened the snaps and revealed my weekly pay-out.

The sight of my money made the tingle grow larger and I began to lose focus. I saw Sheik's face in my mind and I couldn't fight the urge to have someone take me, but it damn sure wouldn't be Corrine. I only mixed business and pleasure when it was money to be gained. I counted the stacks Corrine pushed across the table as she started to explain why she would need more product. She was talking some shit I was trying to hear. More product meant we were doing more business.

"Mami, I have some major moves to make. I got a spot off of Southern Avenue that I have on lock, and I am looking to move a few more bricks through that way. I need to venture out a little more too. There is a drought on the Southside, and I am trying to get these thirsty ass niggas a drink. You feel me?"

I nodded to let her know I was listening, but I was more focused on the neat stacks of cash that were in front of me. I finished my count and placed the bundles into the briefcase I had come in with.

"Expanding with what?" I finally asked after locking my briefcase.

"I was thinking of moving some green through this way. I know you only fuck with that powder, but I know your man Papi got that green."

At the sound of his name I shuddered. I didn't want anyone associating him with me. I knew I could take another angle to get the green so Corrine could expand her growing mini empire. Sheik was known to keep some fire on him. That would be just the excuse to talk to him on the regular.

"That is not my man. I will make some calls and see what I can do for you. I will call you later and let you know what I have worked out." I said.

We walked out through the living area and Corrine's company had switched it up a bit and was engaging in random sex acts on the couch. Corrine all but pushed me out of the door. She wanted to get back to her homemade porno. She gave me a knowing smile and I left. Once I hit my car, I was thinking about Sheik; and more importantly what I was going to do about Papi. I hated when I started thinking about my problems too much because even as a child I didn't handle pressure too well. Bad shit happened when I got into tight situations. I knew I couldn't just make a move on him because I didn't know exactly what he was up to.

CHAPTER 12

Holiday's Bar and Grill
Branch Avenue
Temple Hills, MD

A few months had gone by and I had successfully arranged to buy green exclusively from Sheik. I was officially handling all the business on the Southside. The Parklands and the surrounding areas of Congress Park and The Valley were being locked down. I also had most of Benning Road, Trinidad, and Saratoga on lock too. With the help of Corrine, Southern Ave was well on its way to becoming infested with my brand, and Caesar couldn't be happier. Week by week we were upping our orders, and he respected me bringing him more money than he had seen even while my father had been running shit in the hood on his own.

I hadn't heard too much from Papi. He had tried to call me several times and each time he was forwarded to voicemail. I knew he was pissed. He was mad because I hadn't returned any of his calls and I had also taken over his beloved Saratoga operation. I knew there was going to be blood shed. I was constantly on watch. I always had my heat and Oscar and his goons in tow. Business was going well and I know with me making that kind of money and with haters all around, someone was bound to test my gangsta'.

I was taken away from my thoughts by the sound of my cell phone ringing. I didn't bother to look at the caller ID which I should have.

"Talk to me." I said, answering the call blindly.

"Oh, so now you can talk. I haven't heard shit from you!" Papi said sizzling into the phone.

"Papi, I have been tied up. You know I am busy." I yawned into the phone. I sounded bored and uninterested and I could tell he knew I didn't care about what he had to say.

"YaYa don't fuck with me! I know you have locked down the major areas in the Parklands and most of Benning Road right into NE. You moved right into my fucking spot! Since that pussy was good as a mutha fucka, I am going to let you out easy." He said knowingly.

"What do you mean, 'let me out easy?'" I laughed. "I will get out when I am ready or someone takes me out." I sneered.

"YaYa since we have some past, I will let that shit go. Just return what you owe me and we can go our separate ways." He demanded.

"I don't need any favors from you or anyone else. I am not going to be punked for what's mine. Now you can take this any way you want, but I know your shady ass is trying to set me up and I think we need to end this shit before it gets ugly." I seethed into the receiver.

"Bitch, I got you! Watch your step or you might come up missing. Ain't no trick ass broad gonna' take my work from me. Fuck you YaYa! I'll see you again." He screamed in to the phone. I disconnected the call. I knew I had better get my squad up to speed and make sure Saratoga was on constant watch. If Papi wanted a war, war was what he was going to get. What he didn't know was that I had already been prepared to battle him since I took over Saratoga. I knew that taking over his strip would set off his explosive temper. I think I did it just to spark some shit with him so I could dead him for trying to play me. I didn't want Daddy to know any of the noise Papi's punk ass was trying to make, and I definitely didn't want the streets talking.

*****

NiQue thought I was being careless because I was more focused on going to an album release party for a friend I grew up with named Crack. He was doing big things on the Southside. His artists were making their mark, and niggas were feeling what they had to say. Cap Citi records was doing some damage on the airwaves and they were selling out clubs. I hadn't made it to see Crack's team live, and they were teaming up with another local label, "Free From Bondage." Sun and Starr had an ill flow. I figured I should go ahead and catch them at Gee's because that nigga Dread from Cap Citi was sexy. A sexy nigga like that one could get me to shake my ass any day. I don't know if he was married or not, but fuck it...he was eye candy. It didn't hurt that Crack's team had some ballas with some verbal skills that made me want to show some love.

NiQue felt as though I should be watching the streets and definitely watching Papi. I wasn't even worried about him and his shit. I was ready to go and get my high on. Partying was the mission for the evening. No one was going to stop my flow! Not even Papi's hating ass.

After taking a bath in my over-sized bathtub and softening my skin with my favorite *Bath and Body Works* scent, Cherry Blossom, I put on an emerald green thong and bra set. Then I slid my apple into some dark blue, low-rise jeans. My fresh Kush Girl tee-shirt had the words, "Got Green?" and a large weed plant on the front. My green boots, purse and my signature shades set my outfit off right.

I called NiQue's slow ass, and headed towards my car. It seemed like I couldn't do much of anything without smoking a J, and I had

two rolled. One was for the ride over to NiQue's and the other was
for the ride to the club. I hopped in my Caddy, turned my *Ipod* to
my favorite playlist; and Devin the Dude, and some dude named
Bobby Ray, reminded me of why smoking weed was therapeutic.

I rode down Wisconsin Ave and bucked a left to hit M Street
right through the heart of Georgetown and all of the shops. The
streets were lit up like it was Christmas; inviting tourists from all
over the world. Georgetown was mainly for the wealthy white folks
and tourists who just had to take a piece of DC home with them.
What those same tourists didn't know about Drama City was that
there was a whole different world once you got to the other end of
Pennsylvania Avenue. Once you crossed Potomac Avenue, life was
different. This side is where all you could get from a vendor was
little baggies containing a crack head's dream and all the other shit
that kept my pockets thick.

Once I made it to NiQue's spot, I was a little hesitant pulling
into her row house in Trinidad. I knew I had some shit in my glove
compartment that would sound off real lovely against a nigga's
temple; but my conversation with Papi was clouding my mind like
the thick smoke that filled my car. I shook off the bad feeling and
stepped out of the car into the cool fall breeze. Walking swiftly, and
taking note of everyone around me, I made my way to NiQue's
door. I instantly heard Wale's remix of "Pretty Girls" playing; and
I knew NiQue was not ready to ride out. I rang the bell and was
greeted by Ed, who was NiQue's brother's security. He was just like
family because he worked for NiQue's brother, and on occasion
would travel with Daddy too when he required extra man power.

"Hey Ed." I said giving him a hug; one that lingered a little too
long in my opinion. I knew Ed had a thing for young girls, but I was
hoping he knew where to draw the line. I pulled myself away from
him and headed towards NiQue's second floor. I could feel his eyes
following my ass as it swayed from side to side while I climbed the

stairs. He was just like any other nigga in the street. NiQue was inspecting the finished product in her full-length mirror when I reached her room.

"Bitch you are gonna wind up late to your own damn funeral!" I laughed.

NiQue jumped damn near across the room. She hadn't heard me make my way up the steps because of the music pumping from the speakers that were housed in the ceilings and walls of the upper level of her home.

"YaYa, you scared the shit out of me! Announce ya'self next time!" She said trying to laugh off her fear. That's the kind of shit you went through when you grew up with families like ours. You were constantly watching your back and expecting the unexpected.

"Stop being so damn scary acting." I said taking a seat on the foot of the bed.

"You need to be the one jumping around and shit with Papi gunning for your ass." NiQue laughed nervously.

"That sorry excuse for a hustler called me today on that bullshit. He was acting like he owned the fucking world and everyone in it." I rolled my eyes.

"You are gonna' have to handle him because he isn't gonna just go away quietly. Did you try to reason with him?" NiQue asked me while she was applying her *MAC* lip gloss.

"What do I look like trying to reason with him when he ain't nobody to fear? Fuck him. He is just making noise; trying to be heard. Are you ready to go yet? Crack said he has a spot in VIP for us. I am trying to go out and find my balla' baby!" I said smacking my ass while I wiggled it like a pole dancer. NiQue grabbed her jacket and what she called her "goody bag." That was her bag with her never ending supply of Xtasy pills and already rolled Backwoods.

"Let's make it!" she said and we headed out the door.

We pulled into the already packed parking lot of G's night club.

I had deaded the last of the J we were pulling on and we exited the car. The line was wrapped round the building and heading clear down the block. I sure was glad that I had a nice cushy spot in VIP, and happy that I didn't have to wait in line because I don't do that "waiting" shit either.

I pulled my shades down over my grey eyes and strutted towards the bouncer who was clowning some kid who was trying to get into the club in boots and street wear. The kid was doing everything but promising the burly bouncer a blow job. I strolled over to the bouncer and he waived me and NiQue through after checking his list. When we got inside, the club was packed and it was standing room only from wall to wall. We made our way to the third level of the club and I found our reserved table.

The waitress came with a bottle of *Patron Anejo* and two glasses. She let me know that Crack said the drink was his treat and that he would be over to check me out later. The waitress poured the *Patron* and placed the bottle back in the bucket of ice. I never could understand how a nigga could drink ice cold liquor. I pulled the bottle out of the ice and sat it on the table. I could tell NiQue's "Candy" had kicked in because she was standing and swaying to the music that was booming off of the walls. I was feeling lovely from the piff we had sparked on the way to the club.

I saw Crack and his wife making their way towards our section. They were destined to be a power couple one day. He exuded power and his wife, Queen, was strong. I guess you have to be strong having a mate like Crack who was chasing his dream and wasn't gonna stop chasing until it was his reality. Looking at the two of them made me wonder would I ever have love like theirs. Once NiQue realized we weren't alone anymore, she tried to straighten up because a sister was fried!

"YaYa", Crack said as he moved to hug me. "Glad you could make it out. Finally got you to come out and see what I have been doing with myself all these years! You know my wife Queen; don't you?"

I smiled and extended my hand to her. Nice to see you again." I said, admiring her style. She was dripping in ice. I could tell Crack was doing lovely. His wife was laced in some hot shit I had never seen before.

"Oh, and this is my friend NiQue." I said motioning towards NiQue.

I could tell NiQue wasn't interested in the introductions because she gave them the universal nigga head nod and started bopping to the music again. Wale and TCB were pulsating through the speakers with their song, "Ice Cream Girls." If you weren't from Drama City you couldn't appreciate what Go-Go had to offer.

Crack asked me to join them as they made rounds through the club. NiQue said she was fine chilling in our cushy spot. She was good as long as she had that bottle and her "goody bag." Crack introduced me to all kinds of people he had invested his money in. I mean, he had rappers, actors, and even some authors who wrote that made-up shit about the streets and the so-called struggle. He had endorsement deals, and was promoting his artists' new albums: "Tha Kushilation," "Heat for Tha Streets," "KillZone," and he was working on a project called, "No City for Old Men." Crack was making money hand over fist, and it was all clean money. He even had a company called, "The Kush Boys" who had offered him sponsorship through their Hemp iced tea called, "Chronic Ice." The music changed again, but to a mellower tune.

"Aye YaYa, what do you think about this song? This is one of my newest projects, "Mama's Moonshine." They got that Neo-Soul, Hip Hop thing going on. They are based out of Atlanta.

I nodded my head in approval. They were straight flowing and singing; it was some great "get high music" to say the least. It was on some Erykah Badu meets Andre 3000, and instead of making babies, they made music. I sat thinking of how I could make some of that legal money when Crack broke my train of thought. I looked up into the eyes of the most beautiful specimen of a man I had ever laid my eyes on. He was about 6'3" and had long red dreads that hung down to his waistline. I stood to make his acquaintance.

"YaYa this is Dread, one of my most promising artists. He's been in this music game for a minute. They call him, "Dread the Old Head." This nigga tells a story with the wisdom of a nigga seventy-five years young; with a delivery better than any of these youngin's on the streets or the radio.

I immediately felt my middle moisten. He shook my hand and I could feel the electric spark between us. The nigga was straight off the streets. I could tell he was used to introductions like the one Crack made, and he was definitely used to bitches throwing themselves at him. I could feel him sizing me up. I had to control the shit dead in the tracks before he made the mistake of thinking I was a hood rat.

"Dread what makes you so different from all the other rappers trying to make it?" I asked him just trying to make conversation without seeming thirsty. Dread turned to Crack and had the nerve to laugh at my question.

"Look baby girl, none of these bubble gum, rapping ass niggas got nothing on me. What you think I'm gonna bitch-up and start Souljah Boying out here? I can show you better than I can tell you why I'm going to be the King."

He gave Crack a pound, kissed Queen's cheek, winked at me, and started making his way to the lower level of the club towards the huge stage. Queen was the first to break the silence, she damn near fell over laughing.

"YaYa, don't take him too serious baby girl. He is a hot head by nature. He truly is talented though." she said still giggling. I am glad she saw the humor in the way he had come off on me.

It must have shown that I wasn't used to being carried by dudes before. I could feel my temperature rise. It was rising for the wrong reasons though. I got off on the fact that the nigga thought so much of himself. It made me want to mount up and ride his ass into the fucking sunset. I heard the crowd going crazy on the lower levels. I stepped closer to the banister to look over the crowd below. On the stage was the object of my temporary desire. Dread was rocking back and forth to the bass line of the song, and then he broke out into the hook of the song which was, "Get Me Don't Shit Me." The crowd was losing their mind; screaming the words to the song while Dread ripped the place apart with his lyrical genius. The shit was amazing to see a forty-something rapper doing it way bigger than any main-stream artist to date. He told a story with the swagga of Biggie, but was on his grown man shit like Hova'.

I couldn't believe I was lusting after a nigga who didn't even realize I was fucking street royalty. I pushed him to the back of my mind when NiQue caught up to me. Home girl was sloppy drunk and was being escorted over to me by a few cats I knew from Trinidad. NiQue was staggering and clinging to the banister for dear life.

"Girl, did you hear how that nigga was ripping the mic?" NiQue slurred. She was partying to her own melody in her head and was real touchy feely because she was trying to rub a hole in my arm. That Xtasy had her on a different planet. I could never figure out why she felt the need to chase that kind of high.

"Yeah girl, I heard him." I said trying not to show her how excited I was about meeting him and hopefully seeing him again on a more personal level. Don't get me wrong, I had met some folks in my life time thanks to Daddy and all of his dealings, but this nigga had piqued my interest, or at least for the time being, and then it would be on to the next. That's just how I did things. Foxxy Brown said it best, "Fuck um, check, and on to the next!"

NiQue and I made our way back to our seats after trying to get through the wanna-be's hawking to get into the VIP area. The lights dimmed again, signaling the start of another performance. Dread had taken his place on the stage followed by the rest of Cap Citi and the KushBoys.

"Aye this is why Imma' be King Shawty." Dread spoke into the mic. I knew he was directing that statement towards me. I watched as the performers mesmerized their audience. The big projection type screen was playing the video to the Cap Citi Kush Boys hit song, "Gucci" which featured the actor Jackie Long on the track.

I wanted a piece of Dread and I was going to have some of him. He just didn't know it yet. We were partying hard and doing what NiQue and I do best–tear the club up. We were barely able to make it back to our table when I saw my worst nightmare enter into the VIP section of the club. Before I could even turn to try and go unnoticed, Papi walked right into me. I could feel my pulse quicken and I wasn't sure if it was the anxiety of seeing him or if it was the gallon of liquor I had sloshing around inside of my stomach. Before I could even think of a way out of the inevitable confrontation, Papi was dead on me.

"Aye YaYa. Long time no see." He said coldly. "Is this the way you treat every dude you get with? Fuck him, steal from him, and then try and act like he doesn't exist?"

His eyes were squinted and I could tell he had had one too many drinks too. That mixed with my obvious distaste for him was making for a bad showdown. Fuck the Wild West. It was about to be on and popping and there really wasn't much to stop it either.

"Papi, this is not the time of place for this shit. I am warning you, not tonight!" I tried to walk off calmly like nothing had happened. Apparently, Papi was not going to look like he got played in front of his boys or anyone else for that matter.

"Bitch, you owe me! And now it's time to pay up hoe!" He said, grabbing my arm. NiQue sobered up enough to know that it was about to get ugly.

"Wassup Papi? I haven't seen you in a while. How have you been?" NiQue said with her eyes darting back and forth trying to locate help.

"NiQue mind your fucking business. This is between me and YaYa."

Papi yanked me towards the entrance of the club.

"NiQue, I got this. I am just gonna go and talk to him and settle this shit." I said, not knowing who I was trying to convince – her or me.

In all actuality, I had no idea how I was gonna handle the shit that was about to go down. I was unarmed and I could be walking out of the club to my death. Papi pushed me out into the cool, summer night air, and took my hand so no one passing by would be aware of the trouble that was coming. He led me to his car and demanded that I get in.

"YaYa you are gonna give me my money if you wanna live."

I got into the passenger side and Papi drove off. I had no choice. I was defenseless and my only way out was in the glove box of my own car. I couldn't believe I had gotten caught slipping. If I had listened to NiQue, I wouldn't have been out in the first place and I definitely wouldn't have been in the company of a scrub ass nigga like Papi. The ride towards Baltimore was in silence and I silently prayed that God was listening to my prayers. Papi pulled in front of his home and told me to get out. I slid from the car and slow stepped up the walkway. He opened the door and pushed me inside. Once inside he flipped on the lights, but the whole scene had changed. There were four armed men, two of which were familiar. The two men I had seen in Papi's house before were there again, and apparently they weren't invited to whatever Papi had planned for me.

"Buenos noches. I take it you aren't happy to see me Papi." One of the men said.

Papi started backing up to the door from which we had just come. I could tell the situation was going to get worse. I tried to figure out how I could out of the shit my pussy had somehow gotten me into.

"Juan, I got your money son. This bitch right here has what I owe you. She is the reason I haven't been able to make the math right. This shady bitch has moved into my arena with her father. They are the ones you should be after, not me!" Papi stammered trying to get out of whatever he had gotten himself into.

I must admit it wasn't looking too good for me, but it damn sure wasn't looking good for Papi either. That Juan character didn't look like he cared about what Papi was saying. He motioned for me to come to him. Papi was reluctant to let me go, being that I was his shield. If that mutha fucka let off a shot, I was the only thing protecting Papi from getting smoked in the foyer of his own home. Papi released the grip he had on me. He must have felt like by telling Juan and his goons I was the cause of the money being funny would ensure him his life being spared.

"Chica, are you all he says you are?"

I looked Juan in his eyes and could tell he was about his money. He didn't give a fuck about me or Papi. He just wanted his money. I knew that either way things played out, I wasn't gonna go out like a bitch. I took my stance. "I only took what was there for me to take. He left it out there and I took it." I stated with an attitude.

Juan cracked a smile. "I like this bitch. I knew there was something special about her the first day we saw her. She got balls. I knew she couldn't just be fucking with this lame nigga for nothing." He chuckled at his own joke. What they didn't know was that I had been fucking with him for nothing. His betrayal is what caused me to fuck Papi on his block. It was me being mad for being used. It was just a minor mind fuck which had turned into a great big fuck you. Now, I had plans on fucking Papi big time.

Juan laughed and stepped forward towards Papi. "Well, I see your dick has caused you a problem chico. You got caught slipping and a chick is the one who has you by your balls. Damn homie, did you ever think you would be caught like this? Now, I am going to ask you one more time. Do you have my money? Before you answer, don't gimme no more excuses about your bitch here having it, or her being the cause of you not having my money." He said pointing at me.

Papi squirmed around and was sweating like two mice in a blanket fucking on a hot summer's day. He looked around nervously and began to open his mouth to speak. Before he could utter one word, Juan emptied a clip into Papi's body. His body looked like a life-sized connect the dot game. He was dead before his body even hit the floor. I watched him fall to the floor and didn't even blink. Juan's goons separated and engaged themselves in ransacking Papi's house.

"So you do know your little boyfriend's debt is now your debt. What he owed me, you now owe me."

I rolled my eyes not believing the shit Papi was getting me into even in death. I didn't owe them bammas shit, and I didn't plan on giving them anything. Juan pulled his nine millimeter and aimed it at my head. "You understand what I am saying to you punta?" He asked sternly. I nodded my head up and down slowly, never taking my eyes off of his to show him I wasn't afraid of whatever he threw my way. Juan's thugs had re-entered the hallway and were ready to exit.

"YaYa, you will do what I say. Once we have left I want you to call the police and tell them your boyfriend's home has been burglarized. Tell them you all walked in the door and armed men stormed you at the front door. Other than that, you don't know shit else. Can you handle that?"

"I can handle it." I responded.

"Good, because I would hate to have to mark up that beautiful body of yours!" He said.

The slimy bastard kissed my hand and walked over Papi's bloody, bullet-riddled body, and walked out the door. I ran behind Juan and asked, "What did he owe you?"

"He owed me twenty five G's." He said as he got into his car.

"I know it is chump change for me but, it is the principle. He should have paid me or at least attempted to settle his debt with me."

I was stunned. Twenty-five thousand wasn't shit. Hell, I know Papi had the money, but the cheap bitch just wasn't trying to come up off of it. I walked back towards the house wondering if I should make good on paying Juan, just to keep him out of my hair. Besides, he could have possibly saved my life and didn't know it. If for no other reason than his being at the right place, at the right time, was enough to pay him what Papi owed him. Before calling the Feds, I went through Papi's house and took all that I wanted. I stuffed all that I had collected into the trunk of his car and called the police from my cell phone as Juan had instructed.

The police were there in no time flat and I began crying big crocodile tears. When they found me I was on the floor next to Papi's body like I cared about what had happened. I was weeping for the twenty-five grand I had to pay Juan. Not for the sorry sack of shit that was being carried out in a body bag. The police believed my story of a home invasion because the neighbors told the police that we had just pulled up, they heard the shots, and saw a mysterious truck speed off not long after the gun fire. After a round or two of questioning, I was home free and the police let me leave. I gathered my composure and drove off in Papi's car which was going to be sold to the highest bidder by morning to keep me from having to pay the entire twenty five out of my pocket. I couldn't believe that nigga was costing me money in death.

My thoughts drifted from what had happened to how the hell it had happened. Where the fuck was NiQue? That bitch hadn't even called me to see if I was alive or not.

CHAPTER 13

Big Chair Records
MLK Jr. Avenue
SE Washington DC

The next morning I awoke to my cell phone ringing. "Yeah." I answered groggily into the phone.

"I'm glad to know you are aight girl. What the hell happened with you and Papi? Where is he? NiQue had bombarded me with at least six questions before I could even get a word in edgewise.

"Girl, slow down! I can't talk to you over the phone. Where are you gonna be in about an hour?" I asked her, somewhat annoyed at the fact that she was finally getting around to checking on my wellbeing. Damn near twelve hours had passed since the whole ordeal with Papi, and NiQue hadn't blown up my phone to check on me.

"I am going to get some breakfast at *Denny's* on Benning Road. You can meet me there."

"Aight." I said hanging up before I snapped on her for not being there when I needed her the most.

I swung my feet over the side of the bed and tried to shake off the sleep that was trying to consume me. I had a lot of shit to work out, including what I was gonna do with that nigga's automobile. I don't know what possessed me to keep it instead of calling Daddy or Oscar. I'd much rather not involve them in the minor shit I had going on. I drug myself into the bathroom and started the shower. I let the hot water trickle down my skin which was the perfect treatment for washing my sins and cares away.

My hands started wandering over my body and I realized that I had been so tied up in my work and nonsense that I had no time for play. I massaged my nipples into two hard knots and let my hands roam down to my sweet spot. Closing my eyes, I thought of Dread caressing my slick skin. I imagined it was his hand kneading into my flower. I closed my eyes tighter and I swear Dread was in the shower with me. I heard him say, "Now you can call me King too baby." I exploded all over my hands. I didn't want the feeling to end. I tried to hang on to the fantasy for as long as I could. That is until the water began to get cold. I cleansed my skin and felt like I could handle the shit I had to deal with. I could even deal with talking to NiQue without smacking her for not being a concerned friend. I got dressed and headed out to meet up with her so I could tell her what a crazy ass night I had been through.

When I pulled into the parking lot in front of the *Denny's*, I could see NiQue was already there. Why she was smoking a J in the hot ass parking lot, I will never know. She was always getting smacked. I knew I could smoke a grown man under the table, but NiQue was ridiculous. She spotted me pulling up and a Fed pulling up behind me. She successfully got the J out before he rode past her looking for a space. I swear that bitch needs rehab. I can get into some shit but, she was looking for trouble. Benning Road is not the place to be firing up a J. Especially not in the tiny ass parking lot we were in.

I exited my car and walked towards the entrance. NiQue joined me after spraying herself down with some body spray so she could cover up the weed smell. I am glad she was smart enough to do that because the *Denny's* was a Fed hang out. We waited in the small waiting area and being that it was Saturday morning, it was crowded as all get out in there. Half the waitresses were straight hood rats who all had bad attitudes and the dudes all looked like ex-cons. I know working at *Denny's* couldn't have been their dream job. The shade they were throwing and smug attitudes let you know that they hated their low-paying jobs. Once we were seated, NiQue couldn't wait to start questioning me.

"So, what the fuck happened last night?" She said sounding like a nosy ass teenager.

"Papi took me back to his house." I looked around nervously, hoping no one was listening to us. I doubted if they were because there was way too much going on around us for anyone to hear anything. I started to feel uncomfortable with talking to NiQue about the details. I shrugged off my doubt and continued with the assorted details.

"While we were driving out there he didn't say a word and you know I was shook 'cause I left my tool in the car. Not to mention my blade was under the seat of my ride because I didn't want any hassle from security at the club. When we get to his house he forces me inside. You would never guess what happened when we get inside. I ain't sure if it was a good or bad thing. Papi must have pissed off the free-fucking world because there were dudes inside waiting on him. They shot his ass in front of me. They killed that nigga right in front of me."

"Stop acting like you have never seen a nigga get murked. We did the same shit a few months back or did you forget?" NiQue said menacingly. Her coldness caught me off guard.

"Shhhh bitch. I don't want the whole restaurant knowing all my business." I said trying to get her to bring it down a notch.

"Anyway," I continued. "These niggas killed him and gave me instructions on what I had to do to live. They gave me a way out of the situation with Papi, but now I have to give them the twenty-five G's Papi owed 'em." I concluded. I intentionally left shit out to protect NiQue in case any of the shit came back on me.

"Twenty-five G's is a cake walk for you. Just give it to 'em." NiQue said she wasn't seeing my point.

"Bitch, twenty-five grand is way too much to be spending on that ignorant nigga who was gonna be deaded anyway! I wouldn't want to spend a dime on his sorry behind. I can't even believe you think paying off his debt is a solution." I shot back.

NiQue looked at me in a way I had never seen. She looked disgusted with me. "Life or death, you decide." She said coldly. I sat there dumbfounded and pondered my next move. My thoughts were once again interrupted by the sound of my cell phone ringing. I had a text message from an unknown number. The message was simple and threatening all in one stroke. It read, "Twenty-five grand, one week." I know NiQue could see the change in my attitude, and I didn't feel like explaining what that was about. I wasn't feeling her vibe, but I was going to try and move past it.

"So, what happened to you that you didn't come after me or try and see that I was aight?" I asked.

"I was tied up girl. Literally! After you and Papi left the club, I needed a ride because you were the one that drove, and I was fucked up remember? I had no way to come after you. So, I waited until I saw your boy Crack and his wife Queen. I asked them if they could help me out with a ride. Crack got that dude who was shitting all over the mic, Dread, to run me around the way." At the mention of his name I sat up and hoped that she wasn't going to tell me that she had fucked my latest sexual conquest.

"Girl, he drove me home and let's just say, I thanked him immensely for the ride. Ya' dig?" She laughed.

I wanted to spit in her face. I knew that if that shit with Papi hadn't played out the way it had, I would have been all on that dude

Dread. I played my hate cool though. I didn't want her to see I was upset in the least bit.

"YaYa, that nigga was working with some fiyah down below; you hear me?" She continued.

"So are you going to see him again?" I asked trying to act like I wasn't jealous. She didn't know I was trying to holla, so it wasn't her fault. I started to soften my demeanor a little.

"Aye, I didn't even get his math. I wasn't even trying to get it because I know if he wants this," she said pointing to her stale ass pussy, "He will get up with me. I mean he did take me home so he knows where I live." She finished.

Something in me knew she was being dramatic. That nigga wasn't hardly interested in her groupie ass and I knew it. She was trying to sice it up like it was nothing to her. I knew her better than that. NiQue ain't really have the heart to ask that nigga for his number. She was probably feeling too ashamed to ask him for it after she had given him the punani.

We chit chatted and I was ready to roll. I had had enough of being in that little ass *Denny's* with a million and one things on my mind. NiQue and I agreed to get up with one another later. I told her I had to handle my problem and I rolled out. I was half way to my man Benny's chop shop to try and negotiate a deal with Papi's car when my cell rang again.

"This is YaYa." I answered.

"YaYa, this is detective Gatsby. I am one of the detectives handling your boyfriend Papi's case." I looked at the number and tried to remember to store it in my phone as Private Dick so I wouldn't answer it the next time his nosy ass called. I knew there would be a next time.

"Yes sir, I remember who you are." I said trying to sound sad. After all, my drug dealing boyfriend had been gunned down in his home in front of me less than twenty-four hours ago...or at least that was the story I was trying to sell.

"Yes, ma'am, I was calling to see if there was anything else you could remember about the men who took your boyfriend's life."

That stupid ass detective had no idea my skin was crawling at the sound of someone referring to Papi as my boyfriend.

"All I can remember is all I told you sir." I said sheepishly. We had just come in from a friend of mine's function and when we entered into his home, four armed men bombarded us at the door." I sniffled into the receiver.

"Ms. Clayton, can you remember anything? Something…anything to help us? What were they wearing? Did they speak to you?" He questioned.

"They all wore masks like I told you before. I couldn't see any of their faces. All I remember is that the one who spoke had a thick accent. Detective, honestly Papi was involved in a lot of activity that would piss off Lucifer himself. It could have been anyone. He never involved me in any of his affairs. I never wanted to know more than I did. He said it was better that I knew very little." I started really laying on the tears then.

"Detective, I can't really do this right now. I have a funeral to prepare myself for."

"Ok Ms. Clayton, I understand. If you can think of anything, please don't hesitate to contact me."

I promised him that I would call him if I could remember anything that I hadn't already told him. I knew I looked like a suspect. Who the fuck walks into a hail of gunfire and walks away untouched? I continued out of the city and headed into Prince George's County to Greenbelt where Benny owned a warehouse district. Inside his warehouses he stored all of the hot cars he had some of his boys lift from the street. Benny had a whole operation going from top to bottom. Within the docks of the warehouses were all kinds of cars; foreign and domestic. Luxury vehicles and exotic; it didn't matter. Whatever you needed, Benny had it, and he also had his wife's family in place at the DMV to make sure that you could easily register the vehicle with no problems.

Benny owned a fleet of tow trucks. If you watch the news on the DMV, chances are you have heard about the mysterious happenings of folks having their cars towed away in the middle of the night. Yeah, well Benny had everything to do with it. His goons would case out places, find whatever vehicle suited their fancy, load them onto the flatbed tow trucks and roll out with them. I knew getting rid of Papi's Lex was nothing for Benny. It was easy and clean. He and his guys didn't have to run the risk of some angry car owner busting one at their asses for their car.

Once I drove around to the loading docks where Benny had told me to meet him, there were some guys smoking cigarettes and talking shit. I cut the engine on my car and got out. Just as I was trying to decide which one of the greasers I was going to ask to go get Benny, he walked out of the docking bay.

'YaYa what it do?" He said walking towards me with a big grin on his face. You would think he was eyeing me, but he was really peeping the car.

You see Benny is just like Nicholas Cage in "Gone in Sixty Seconds." He had much love for the cars he lifted. He had some kind of relationship with them. I almost felt sorry for his wife. She always came in second next to a car.

"Hey Benny. You can stop drooling over my car; my baby is not for sell." I said. The car I got for you is a Lexus 430. You can send your folks to get it today.

Benny's eyes widened at the sound of a Lexus. "What you want for it YaYa? Better yet, what's wrong with it? Ain't nobody just gonna' give away a Lexus that ain't got no problems."

"Look it was my boyfriend's car and he got murked last night. I need the money to handle his funeral arrangements." I lied. Benny knew what my family was about and he knew damn well that I didn't have to sell a car for some bread, but hearing that my boyfriend got murked seemed to erase any reservations Benny had. Just like that I gave him the address to my house where he could pick up the car. I told him where the keys would be and everything. He gave me ten grand for the car and gave me an extra five for it being a no hassle transaction. I was more than half way to my goal of twenty-five thousand. I guess some was better than none. I would go and retrieve the rest of the money and give the mysterious men with revenge and murder on their minds, what they felt was rightfully theirs.

I hadn't seen too much of my father and Neko lately and spending time with them meant a lot to me all of a sudden, being that my life could have ended last night. I figured I would take them out for dinner at the Gaylord at The National Harbor. I heard the food was pretty good and there was a lot to do at the Harbor. I pulled into the garage of our home and saw that Papi's Lexus was still parked in front of our home. I hopped out of my car and walked back to the driveway and popped the trunk of the Lexus. I don't know what made me do it, but I felt like going through the car was in my best interest before Benny's people's arrived to take it.

What I saw nearly knocked the wind out of me. The trunk contained four black leather bags. Two of them contained raw uncut cocaine and the other two bags contained neat stacks of cash that was bundled up. I looked around because I was out in the open and I knew I wasn't always as alone as I had felt. I slammed the trunk closed on the car, hopped in the driver's seat, cranked up the engine, and pulled the car into the garage next to my own car to inspect the contents of the Lexus in private. Unbeknownst to me, I had good reason to move the car to the garage because I most certainly was not alone.

CHAPTER 14

The Legend Nightclub
Naylor Road
Temple Hills, MD

Detective Gatsby sat in his unmarked cruiser across from the Clayton home, eating a glazed donut and sipping re-heated 7-Eleven coffee. His partner, Detective Lockley, was sitting in the car with him, playing around on the laptop that was mounted into the car's console. Gatsby hadn't had a good feeling about the details of the case and decided that maybe they should watch the coming and goings of the late, Trevor "Papi" Yosemen's girlfriend, YaSheema.

He knew there was more to the whole story than what the girl was telling. It could have been out of fear, or it could have been because she didn't want anyone knowing what had really happened when the dearly departed met his demise. He had her tested for gunpowder residue and she checked out clean. Not so much as a spatter of blood was found on her clothing. He just couldn't figure out why, if Papi had been shot in cold blood in front of her, had the killers left a witness. Twenty years on the force had taught him to always follow his gut. When he pulled the Clayton woman in the room for questioning, something about her didn't sit well with him, and he wanted to get the truth out of her. She was cold as ice. That too could have been one of two things making him uneasy about her. Either she was hiding something or shock had set in. Something about the beautiful grey-eyed black girl intrigued him.

Gatsby sat looking out of the window towards the Clayton home hoping that the girl really didn't have anything to do with the murder of her boyfriend. He really wanted to see what she felt like. He had always had a thing for black chicks, but being that he was from a very strict Italian upbringing, fucking niggas was definitely forbidden in his world. Sure he had nothing against black people, and had even been in love with a chick from Haiti who made him happy to come home to and see her face everyday. Only she wanted more from him than he could offer. She wanted acceptance into his entire world, which meant his family. There was no way he could bring a nigga before his father and proclaim his love for her to him. There would be blood shed if he even thought of doing so.

Just like all good things in life they come to an end. Anona was not feeling being kept as his little dark secret, and decided that she would rather return home to Haiti instead of being a prisoner of love. Anona had returned for visits to the States frequently, and had returned with good news on her last visit. She was pregnant from her last visit three months before. Gatsby was excited and didn't give a damn about what his family thought of who he decided to be with. All he cared about was pleasing Anona and being a good father to his child. Gatsby and Anona had planned on sharing their good news with his family. He had forewarned Anona about their hostility towards blacks, and how he would be out casted and shunned because of their wicked and nasty ways.

Being that Donald Gatsby was his parent's only son, the news of the nigger baby wasn't received well. His mother could barely control herself. She walked around the large dining table they were all seated at during dinner, and she smacked Anona so violently that she saw stars before her. Anona pushed herself away from the table; too stunned to react. Gatsby moved in to help her stand so they could gather their things and be done with his family forever. If they could not accept his new family for who they were, then fuck them all. As they exited his childhood home for what he knew was the last time, Gatsby unleashed every vile feeling he had for his parents.

"Hell has a place just for the two of you in it!" He yelled at them while ushering Anona out of the front door and down the drive way.

"You are a disgrace to the family and you wait and see, that nigger ain't gonna do nothing but bring you trouble. That mixed breed baby will be cursed and so will everything you touch." His father shouted back.

His mother was acting like a mad woman screaming and crying on the front lawn. She was throwing things all about. "She put that voodoo curse on you. She made him her slave." She hollered out. Gatsby got them to the car safely without being hit by any of the projectiles his mother was launching from the front porch.

Anona had been warned of his family's behavior and had pushed him into the unfortunate experience. She felt guilty and wasn't in the best of spirits, even though Donald told her that he didn't need them in his life. He told her she was his everything and their world would be complete as long as she and the baby were in it. Over the next few weeks Anona started coming out of her depression. She was starting the process of moving herself back to the States so that she and Donald could be married. There wasn't a day that went by that Gatsby didn't think or feel he had made the right decision. Anona was his life, and he would do anything to appease her. He needed her unconditional love to survive. She gave him pure happiness, which was something he was not accustomed to.

The weeks turned into months, and his soon to be wife and unborn child held his undivided attention. Their wedding was days away. It was nothing extravagant, just an intimate affair among friends and Anona's family. Some of his sister's had agreed to be there and did not care what race their baby brother was marrying. As long as Anona treated him right, and did right by their baby, they vowed to remain by their brother's side. On the day of the wedding Anona was rushing around trying to take care of last minute preparations. She told Donald she had errands to run and would meet him to be his new bride.

Donald continued on with getting himself prepared to become the perfect husband that he knew he could be. He left for the church in good spirits. When it was time for his blushing bride to walk down the aisle, she missed her queue. She had left him standing there. No reasons or explanations were given. Donald sat at the church hopelessly for hours awaiting Anona. The guests had all left and Donald couldn't understand why she had left him there alone when that morning she seemed so happy to be his wife. Donald's anger slowly turned into fear. He knew Anona wouldn't just leave him like that. A thousand different scenarios played out in his head as he left the church and headed home. He began thinking what if she had gone into labor? What if she had been hurt? He drove through the streets of upper Northwest like a bat out of hell. Gatsby was hoping against hope that she and his baby were alright.

Gatsby pulled up in front of the home he had shared with Anona and was relieved to see her car out front. He ran through the front door calling her name. Anona didn't respond. He began to taste the vile of fear creep up from the pit of his stomach and into his throat. He pulled his service revolver and crept up the steps that lead to the bedrooms. The master bedroom door was slightly ajar. Gatsby pushed open the bedroom door and could not believe the horror he found.

His bride was lying on the floor at the foot of the bed with her body contorted like a circus side show freak. She was lying there in her wedding gown which was no longer white; it was a bright shade of crimson. The worst part of it was that her dress was pulled up over her pregnant belly, and carved into her stomach were the words, "Nigger bitch."

There was no denying that she had died a horrible death, and there was no doubt by whose hands it had been caused. Gatsby sat there just holding his bride's bloody corpse. He was rocking her back and forth. His fellow boys in blue found him just like that, holding Anona staring blankly at the wall. It had taken him months of therapy and numerous evaluations before he was able to deal with the pain of loosing the love of his life and his unborn baby. Anona had been beaten and raped so badly that their baby girl had no chance of survival against their attacker. Gatsby played the game the doctors wanted him to play. After his wife and child were laid to rest, he made them believe that he was sane and that he was healed of the wrath that had been looming inside his soul.

Once he was released back into society and had returned to work, he had his mind set on revenge. It didn't matter who he had to kill, as long as the death of his love was avenged. He knew who did it and he knew why. No one else cared that she was black, no one else but his mother and father. They would rather go to jail and burn in hell before they let their only son marry a black girl. He knew that Anona and their baby girl, Naylah, couldn't rest until he had set their souls free by killing the very people who had destroyed his fairytale.

Weeks of planning had gone into how it would be done. Donald snuck into his parent's home when he knew their tired, old asses would be asleep. He crept into their room where they slept in two separate beds like the old fashion biddies they were. He swung the metal bat against his mother's head first, causing a sickening thump that sounded like a watermelon being dropped from five stories down to the pavement. She never even knew what was happening. She was dead before she could fully wake. Donald's father stirred from the commotion, and could barely sit up before his son descended upon him.

"You no good son of a bitch. You took my whole world from me because you can't accept people. So you see your dead wife over there? You will be joining her in hell. Donald had taken hold of his father around the throat and forced him to look at his dead wife's bloody, battered body. Her head was a heap of mush, and the elder Gatsby couldn't bear to look at her.

"Look at her mother fucker!" Donald screamed. "Do you know what it felt like to walk in on your dead wife's body? Well, I guess now you can know what it feels like!" His father sobbed his wife's name over and over again.

"Oh, GiGi. What have I done to you? Oh, GiGi, please forgive me." He cried.

"Oh, you want that dead bitch to forgive you? What about me? How about you beg for my forgiveness?" Gatsby said as he released his grip from around his father's neck. He pushed him back into a laying position on the bed and ripped away his pajama bottoms.

"Do you know what it's like to be violated?" He flipped the old man over face down and began brutally raping the old man with the baseball bat that was covered in his dead mother's blood.

Gatsby slipped into a state of metal unstableness, and couldn't control his actions. He just wanted his father to feel the pain that he had inflicted upon Anona. Gatsby had been so deep in thought about Anona and Naylah that he hadn't realized that his father had passed out. The only thing that brought him to his senses was the smell of the blood and shit that was now covering the bat. He quickly removed the bat and rushed to the bathroom, careful not to touch anything in any of the rooms. He began cleaning the bat and wiping down anything he had touched. When he had re-entered his parent's bedroom, his father was semi-conscious and moaning in agony. Gatsby rushed to his side and pulled the gun he had brought with him to finish the job. He shook his father until he parted his eyes.

"Did you do it Dad?" Gatsby asked his father holding the gun tight in his hands.

His father was barely audible. He was slipping in and out of consciousness. Gatsby shook him again and asked his father again, "Did you kill my wife and daughter?" His father smiled a sickening smile and shook his head up and down.

"Yeah, I killed them and if I woulda' known that black bitches had good pussy like that, I would have had me some of that years ago too. Fuck you!" The old man sputtered. That almost drove Donald crazy. He placed the nine millimeter to the old man's temple and told him to enjoy purgatory, the he pulled the trigger.

That had been ten years ago. Thinking back on it felt like someone had opened the wounds and poured salt into them. Gatsby never regretted killing his parents. He didn't regret burning their half-a-million-dollar home to the ground, and walking away like ain't shit happen. If he had it all to do again, he would. Anything for Anona and Naylah.

Gatsby sat up when he saw YaSheema pull up into the driveway. He watched her walk back down the driveway to the Lexus that had been at the crime scene the night before. She popped the trunk and examined the contents inside. Apparently, whatever was in the trunk was something that she didn't care to share with the rest of her prestigious Georgetown neighbors, because the way she looked around surveying her surroundings warned Detective Gatsby that something was inside that car that he wanted to see. She hopped in the car and moved it into the garage and closed the mechanical doors behind her and the cars.

Gatsby sunk back into his seat. His partner had missed the whole damn scene because she was too busy *Facebooking* to care about what was going on with the Clayton girl. Gatsby knew there was more to it than YaSheema was letting on, but he would be there when she either slipped up or was ready to tell the truth. Gatsby had had enough of watching the girl for the day. He decided he would call it quits, head to his empty home, and drown his sorrows and misery with a bottle of whatever he had in his liquor cabinet. He pulled his unmarked car from the curb just as the tow truck pulled up into the driveway.

Chapter 15

The Cross Roads Nightclub Bar and Grill
Peace Crossing
Hyattsville, MD

I had taken all of the bags out of the car and discovered that Papi was holding some major figures in the trunk. I had also pulled out all of the stuff I had taken from his house. There was over five hundred thousand dollars bundled in those stacks. There was more coca in the car than I cared to put my hands on, but I knew I had to get it out of there before Benny's boys came to scoop up the car.

I removed ten grand out of the stacks and thought how lucky I was to not have to come out of pocket on any of the shit going down. Not only did my Papi situation get handled, but the money issue with his killer had resolved itself as well. I sent a text to Juan and let him know that I had retrieved all of the money and he sent me a reply telling me where to meet him to drop it off. I wasn't happy about having to see him again, but if I wanted to be rid of him and not bring anymore drama, then I knew I had better meet him. I decided for that for the transaction, I wasn't going to go alone. I was going to take Pinky with me just in case Juan wanted to go back on his word.

Pinky was this broad who worked for Daddy every now and again. She was just as ruthless as any nigga on the streets. She may have been worse because she didn't look like a threat. She looked like your average hood bitch. You would never guess she was packing heat. I didn't have to get up with Juan until later in the evening and I had already hipped Pinky to my plan, so I had some time to kill. I went to the rec room and found Neko playing a game on the *PS3*.

"Hey boy, what you up too?' I asked him.

"Nothing just playing *Madden*. Why? What you got planned?"

"I was thinking maybe we could go out and do something. Maybe go eat. Have you seen Daddy?" I inquired.

"Naw, I haven't seen Pop since earlier. We had breakfast and you know how he do."

"Oh well, are you game for going out to eat? Daddy is going to have to catch us on the next trip."

"Yeah, as long as you're paying, I am eating." He laughed.

I stood in the rec room and looked at my little brother and admired him. He was becoming a fine young man and I was so proud of him. My mother could never afford him the things that Daddy and I could. I guess he could feel me staring at him.

"Why are you standing there grinning at me?" He quizzed.

"I am looking at you because you are me, smart ass." I laughed.

He had the same stormy grey eyes as I did. I guess that was the only thing our no good ass Momma gave us. Or so I thought. We rolled out to the Harbor to enjoy each other's company.

"YaYa, what was it like growing up like this?" Neko asked over dinner.

"What do you mean, 'like this?'?" I quizzed.

"I mean with all the money and all the stuff that Pop has. I have never had anything. Christa ain't care about what happened and she only lived to get high." He said.

"I never really took the time to think about what life would have been like if I didn't have money. I mean, Daddy didn't make his money like most folks do, so life was different. I guess life has been good. It is much better now that I have you in it." I said truthfully.

"Well, I am glad that I have you now because Christa wasn't shit and I know she was going to lead me down a path of destruction. Whatever happened to her YaYa? Did she really just leave me with ya'll?"

"Neko, she was no good to any of us. She had to go. I asked her to leave and she left. I guess she went on to get high and just kept going. I told her she could do anything she wanted with herself, but she was not going to include you in the equation and she left."

I could not believe I had lied to him about where his no count ass mother was, but he was better off not knowing anymore than that.

"Well, whatever her reason for rolling out, I sure am glad she left me with you." He smiled.

Neko and I talked more about how he was excited about starting a new school and the friends he had made. We talked so much that I almost forgot about the business I had to tend to. I had forty-five minutes until it was time to meet up with Juan and Pinky. I decided to just take Neko with me because it was no way I was going to be able to make it across town and back in enough time. All I wanted to do was get Juan out of my hair and the sooner the better. Pinky hit me on my cell and let me know she was in route to where we were supposed to meet Juan. Neko and I were already in the car listening to the CD Crack had given me.

I was a little nervous taking Neko with me; but I had no other choice. I whipped around the beltway to Capital Heights to the Addison Road metro station Juan told me to meet him at. I got there ten minutes before I was to meet Juan. As soon as I parked, I saw Pinky dismount her hot pink Ducati. When Pinky hopped off her bike and removed her helmet to reveal a head full of hot pink locks with blond tips, I could see Neko staring her down like if he could jump into her pants, he would. I had to admit Pinky was the truth. She was stacked from head to toe. She was beautiful, and she almost made me envious of the fiyah she possessed. Although she was beautiful, she was also very deadly. Quick to cock, aim, and shoot. That's why I knew she had to come along because where some niggas would bitch up; Pinky wasn't scared to make her Nina clap. Best of all, she didn't look like an assassin and no one would expect it coming from her 5'4" frame. Her high yellow skin glowed and it was speckled with the cutest brown freckles. Her outwardly appearance gave her a youthful teenage look that would make niggas suspect she was more of an overly-developed eighteen year old than a twenty-eight year old killer.

I told Neko to wait at the car for me and no matter what happened; he was to stay in the car unseen. He wanted to question me, but I gave him a look that said that it wasn't the time for Q and A. I walked over to Pinky with my *Gucci* heels clicking against the pavement with every nervous step I took. I patted the small of my back with my right hand to make sure "Chase" was where she should be in case shit got sticky. I wasn't going to be caught without her again. I carried the money in my left hand. I was surveying my surroundings cautiously behind my *Dolce* frames that hid me eyes from outsiders who tried to enter the doorway to my soul. Pinky and I joined each other and walked about twenty paces to where I was to meet Juan. As I was filling her in on the exchange, a white Mercedes CLS 550 pulled up in front of us. The window rolled down just enough for me to see Juan's face peek over the opening.

"Hola Mami." Juan said with a *Chester the Molester* type smile. That shit made me uneasy, and made the hair on the back of my neck stand to attention.

"Hello." I said in a low monotone just trying to hurry the shit along because I ain't trust Juan one bit, and I think Pinky felt it because she reached for the briefcase that was in my hand.

Pinky stepped up to the car with her long dreads hanging down her curvy frame. She extended the briefcase to the opening in the car and Juan shook his head.

"YaYa, my dear we did not discuss you bringing company. No matter how beautiful the company is, this punta should not be approaching me." Juan said addressing me.

As if Juan pushed the button in Pinky's mind that screamed, *kill a nigga,* she pushed the briefcase in my chest and pulled her Nina from her side holster under her pink *Harley* jacket. It was all done in one swift, fluid movement. It was obvious that Juan didn't know he was fucking with a trained killer and he flinched at the sight of the steel that he was staring down the barrel of.

"Juan I assure you that you do not want to make an enemy of Pinky." She is a good girl, but she can be a very bad girl if need be." I said handing the briefcase to him. All the while Pinky did not lower her aim from Juan's face.

"I think you will find all of what you are expecting is there and we should never cross paths again. I even want to thank you for the service you provided for my family for that 'thing' you did."

Juan looked as confused as a mentally-challenged three year old that had just had a set of algebraic equations put in front of him.

"I see you are confused. Maybe I should fill you in. Papi was no friend of mine. Actually, he was an enemy and he was definitely on his way out; whether you did it or I did it, he was done. I guess you didn't do your homework on who you were fucking with? I am sure my father wouldn't appreciate you threatening me and making me pay Papi's debt. But since you came along at the right time, I figured I would entertain you by giving you what you asked for. Juan, please don't ever disrespect me or my business associate again." I said.

Juan finally found the balls to speak up. "And just who is your father and why should I care about who he is?" He sneered.

"Darnell Clayton. Is that enough to make you understand the caliber of bitch you are fucking with?" I responded sparking a *Djarum* cigar.

I watched Juan's face frown up and fidget in his seat. He didn't look too happy to know that he was being one-upped by a female. I started to realize that most of these dudes didn't like to be showed up by a bitch. Maybe it was an ego thing. No matter what it was, they had better deal with it because I was here to stay. I wasn't going anywhere unless someone toe tagged my ass. Pinky still hadn't forgiven Juan for his disrespect. She kept her aim trained on his dome and wasn't going to drop her piece until she either got the apology she wanted, or she did his ass.

"Look YaYa, I want no problems with you or your family. Let's just forget all of this happened. We are done here." He said unsure of how to get out of the bullshit he had placed himself in. He closed the briefcase and was getting ready to make an exit when Pinky let off round after round into the car. She lit up that car like the Fourth of July. Juan's driver had holes in his chest the size of golf balls. Juan's head was no more.

Pinky calmly reached on what was left of Juan's lap and removed my briefcase. She handed it to me. I released the latches and handed her all the money inside the briefcase. I smirked knowing it was money well spent! There was no way I was going to let Juan live! She gave me a knowing nod and walked calmly back to her bike, pulled on her helmet, mounted her pink motorcycle, and exited the garage. I started walking back to my own vehicle quickly and saw what I had forgotten. My baby brother was watching me looking shook like he was next up on my hit list. I slid in the driver's seat and started the engine.

"Here hold this." I said handing him the briefcase. I pushed on the gas and drove out of the garage because I was sure the whole damn city of Capital Heights heard them hot ones sound off.

Once we got out of the garage safely, I instructed Neko who sat motionless in the passenger seat, to wipe down the briefcase. I pulled out a J of Kush from the ashtray and sparked it up. I thought about what I was going to say to Neko. I figured, *sorry little brother for exposing you to a murder* wasn't going to cut it.

"Neko, I didn't mean for you to ever see anything like that. Shit just happened and Pinky ain't to be fucked with. She has a hot head. I'm…I'm sorry." My voice trailed off as I inhaled the thick smoke from the blunt. I exhaled the smoke and my mind drifted to thoughts of how my Dad had introduced me to this game. It wasn't quite as harsh, but I did get brought into the game to serve my purpose and maybe Neko was brought in to serve his. Maybe by some sick twist of fate, it was meant for him to be present for the events of the day. Maybe it was time for him to get his feet wet.

Neko just nodded his head up and down as if it were all cool. We rode in silence all the way to Georgetown. I caught him watching me from time to time as though he were with a complete stranger. I hated the looks he gave me. It made me feel unclean. True bill, I didn't even know what I had unearthed by exposing my brother to my murder and mayhem. I said it before. Christa bred a killer in me. Who knew her DNA was so powerful? It was like I had added fuel to a smoldering fire. Neko was hungry to know all about the "Family Business" and would not take no for an answer. It was like murder woke him up and turned him on. Instead of all the things we talked about that fateful day, he did the opposite. He wasn't interested in school and his friends. He wanted to go to the gun range and run the streets. He was smoking weed and staying out all night. He lost interest in his art and was constantly on my ass about putting him on. How could I deny him a taste of the streets?

Speaking of the streets, they were talking and my name was ringing bells in them muthafuckas. Niggas and bitches both knew I was, "that bitch," and I wasn't gonna' let anyone or anything get in my way of making money. Pinky's actions had just further boosted my reputation. I was loving it! It was like riding an orgasm out until I was spent from the passion.

CHAPTER 16

Island Café
Upsher Street
NW Washington, DC

I was about seven pulls into my J when my cell phone began vibrating on the table next to me. Lazily, I looked at it and wondered why NiQue didn't have any other friends outside of me to bother early on a Saturday morning.

"Yo, what it do?" I answered.

"Nothing girl, just let Dread out the door. I told you that nigga would make his way back over to get some of this good good." NiQue giggled. "That nigga can flow like shit girl. I might make him my man. He just told me that he just got signed. He and a few of his other boys that fuck with Cap Citi Entertainment just got the green lights for the mainstream. " She continued.

"Maybe we could both fuck with some big time rappers." She said excitedly.

I shook my head and let out a plume of smoke. I was not interested in hearing the torrid details of her session with who was supposed to be my play thing. Nor was I interested in her trying to make plans to become that man's girl. I knew he only fucked her because I had mysteriously disappeared. NiQue most likely threw the pussy at him sideways and he didn't know she was my friend. I listened to her babble on and on until she mentioned Sheik.

"Wait you saw Sheik last night? Where did you see him?"

"See now I know you weren't listening to anything I said to you because I just told you I saw him up at Black's Carwash on Florida Avenue. Apparently, Dread and Black are boys and Dread went to get his ride cleaned. When we were pulling out of the carwash, I saw Sheik. He spotted me and asked me where your black ass was." She laughed.

"NiQue, I don't ever listen to your ass girl because you never make any damn sense. Now what did Sheik say he wanted?"

"He just asked me where you were and if I would tell you to call him. He said he got some more business for you." She said.

I sunk back into the bed feeling defeated. He didn't want me, he wanted to handle business. I hadn't been fucked in over a month. The last piece of dick I had was dead and gone and wasn't coming back. Maybe that was what was wrong with me. I had been real snappish and ready to squabble with anyone who wanted to try me. Lack of sex could make me an evil bitch. NiQue was still going on and on in my ear, and I had no clue what the fuck she was saying. I decided I was going to interrupt her and try to get her to go out with me.

"Damn, Motor Mouth. Can I get a word in edgewise?" I said.

"You think you can stay off of that dude's dick long enough to go out with me tonight? Girl, I haven't had any form of sex since our dearly departed Papi. I have to find a replacement." I said.

I told her I would call her later after I found something hot to wear. After all, I was on a mission to get a plaything until I got up with, *Mr. Sheik the Real Thing.* I deaded the J and swung my legs over the side of the bed and stood up. I turned to face the mirror that was on the adjacent wall. My chocolate skin was glowing and my body wasn't a size six, but I got hips and curves that will make a nigga sick.

I loved me all over. I was ready for someone to love me all over too. I got dressed and headed down the hall to check on Neko. That lil' nigga was really getting beside himself. He was staying out late and I know he was getting higher than gas prices.

I let myself into his room without knocking and there was my baby brother standing upright with some little tramp seated on the edge of the bed with his dick lodged down her throat. Neko had his head thrown back in ecstasy with his hands planted firmly on the back of the girls head. He was so busy thrusting in and out of her mouth that he didn't even see me. I was glad he hadn't seen me too because that would have been real awkward. I backed out of Neko's room and headed for the steps. Right before I grabbed the handle to leave out the door, I reminded myself to have a serious talk with my baby brother about hood chicks and bringing them to the house. I also reminded myself to grab him some rubbers because a baby was something none of us were ready to have. I turned the handle and Daddy was standing on the other side of the front door.

"Hi Daddy! I feel like I haven't seen you in ages." I sang, pulling him in for a hug. I then noticed something was very wrong because my father didn't hug me back. He barely acknowledged my presence in front of him. I immediately stepped back and examined his worried face.

"Is there something going on that I need to know about Daddy?" I asked him with fear mounting.

Daddy tried to smile and tell me there was nothing to worry about. He tried to tell me that he was just tired and still had some business to take care of before he could settle in for a mid-day nap. I knew he wasn't telling me everything. Over the years I got used to my father being elusive and secretive. It was just a part of who he was and what he did. He stepped into the house and I stepped back in with him. He was holding a piece of paper in his hands and was not trying to let me see what was on it. I decided I wasn't going to pester him with questions about what was really going on and why he looked shook. I just let him know that Neko had company and that I was going to step out for awhile. I gave him the weekly numbers since it was the first time I had seen him in week. We never kept the same time and hours. We had both gotten so busy, we barely crossed paths. If it weren't for Neko giving me status updates on Daddy, I would never know what was going on with him.

I kissed my father's cheek and tried to steal a glance of the solitary sheet of paper that looked to be the source of his worry. He pulled the paper out of my reach and sight when I went to kiss him. I headed out the door, finally making it to the car, and pulling out of the driveway. I figured I wouldn't go too far to shop. The Solbiato shop was only a little ways down the block. I found a space, although I was kicking myself for driving down the block. The parking in Georgetown was horrendous. It would take a solid hour to just find someplace to park at times. I found a space because it was early and the serious shoppers hadn't hit G-town yet. I knew it wouldn't be too long before the die-hard shopping fanatics would be flooding the overly populated streets. I walked into the shop and was drawn to the bright colors. That was the "in thing" for the summer; bright clothes and shoes.

I saw a tall man in the corner of the store that appeared to work in the shop. I needed him to get an item off of the wall that I wanted to try on. As I approached him, I saw he was definitely not an employee. What caught my attention was the design on the back of his shirt. It was the logo for Cap Citi. Either the dude was on Crack's team or he had just purchased the shirt from somewhere. Either way, the shirt was sick and I wanted one. I knew Neko would like it. It was a picture of the U.S. Capital and it had flames surrounding it. The words under the Capital set in flames said, "We make this Citi Hot!"

"Excuse me, but where can I get a shirt like that?" I asked the dude wearing it.

He turned to face me and he took my breath away. He was tall. I mean really tall. He stood about 6'6" and had long soft hair that was pulled into a ponytail. I silently wished that I knew how to braid hair. Especially if that meant that fine ass nigga would be between my legs. His skin was smooth and even, and his eyes were inviting.

"You can get them off of my label's website." He answered.

Damn, maybe I didn't have to go to the club to find *Mr. Right Now*. I think *Mr. Right Now* had run into me.

I finally spoke up. "Oh, so you are signed to Crack's label?" I asked.

He gave me the once over and was surprised to see that I knew who Crack was.

"Oh, so you know my people then huh?" He asked.

"I might." I laughed.

"Well, it sounds like you know more than most. But you can get the shirts from the website." He said and then turned to finish his task of sifting through the jeans.

"Well, thank you for the information...Ahhhh, I didn't catch your name." I said hoping he wasn't going to just end the conversation like that. I was interested in seeing him naked and he was going to allow me that opportunity.

"The name is Nato but you can call me Jo." He offered.

"May I ask how you got Jo from Nato?" I asked trying to keep the conversation going.

"My stage name is Nato and that is short for *Niggas Are Taking Over*. Jo is my name." He said smiling.

His smile was infectious and I smiled up at him, hoping he could sense that I wanted him to take me in the dressing room and fuck me. I learned that Jo was one of the newest members of

The Cap Citi label and was well on his way to being what The Cap called, "God's Gift." We stood in the store and talked for awhile.

"Well Miss…you never gave me your name." He said looking me over again.

"You never asked for it, so I ain't offer it." I said real cocky like. "Since you want to know…my name is YaYa."

"So, YaYa, do you have plans this evening? I would like to get to know you better."

I remembered that I had already made plans with NiQue.

"Yeah, I have plans to go out with my girl. We planned on hitting up the club." I informed him.

"Well, are you busy now? I have to go to the studio and handle this music thing and then I am free. Why don't you go with me and then we can get lunch or something?"

I wasted no time accepting his offer and decided that going with him was a better option than sitting alone at home with Daddy, who was in his own world; or Neko, who was sure to be into something if he was even home. I purchased my items and walked out of the store with Nato. We headed to my car, since he didn't drive, and I followed his directions to a neighborhood Southeast. Once we pulled up in front of our destination, I cut the motor off and exited the car following NATO's moves. We walked up the steps to a house that sat right on MLK Jr. Avenue. He used his keys and opened the doors to the Cap Citi recording studio. The entrance was painted red and there were all sorts of framed pictures of Crack and Dread and various other people posing with stars. Dread was in one of the pictures with a mean mug on his face, giving Mark Wahlberg a pound. There were pictures of Crack with celebrities like Dr. Dre and the famous pimp, Bishop Don Juan.

I was amazed that Crack was doing so well. It looked as though he was eating good and so was everyone around him. I paused to check out a few more pictures of Dread and couldn't figure out why I was so taken by him. Even though I was standing there with a handsome specimen of a man, I couldn't help but be envious of NiQue. We walked further into the house and the living room area was a reception area. Nato explained that there was a receptionist that worked there Monday through Friday. They were using the studio for themselves and renting it out whenever the Cap Citi artists weren't using the studio. They had a very nice hustle going on and I respected it.

We walked down some steps and into a sitting area. You could tell it was where all the magic happened. There was a booth and a separate room for the sound engineers equipped with top-of-the-line sound equipment. There were some guys seated in plush chairs and some hood rat looking groupies seated with them. There were thick plumes of smoke coming from the rotation of Js that were being passed around the room in a cipher. The men were freestyling, trying to impress the chicks that were obviously thirsty for them. The men all acknowledged me and Nato, then they went back to their lyrical battle. Out of a room from the back walked Crack, Dread, and some other dude who had a thick African accent. They were laughing and talking when they noticed they had a new guest in their presence.

I hugged Crack. "I guess I was more interested in your business than you think." I laughed.

"YaYa what brought you here? Or should I even ask?" He said looking from me to Nato smiling.

"So, we meet again shawty." I heard Dread say. His voice commanded attention with it's deep smooth baritone.

I snapped out of the trance I was in from seeing him again. I remembered that he had just fucked my best friend a few hours before. Nato asked me was I cool, and I let him know Crack was like family so he headed towards the booth to lay a track for an upcoming mixed-tape. Crack informed us that he and Queen had plans on meeting a few investors over dinner and he left. I took a seat and Dread found a seat next to me just as a pretty brown skin girl with hazel eyes walked down the steps. She rushed in the room issuing apologies for her tardiness. She introduced herself as Kimya.

"Ain't nobody thinking bout you Kim. You're always late for a session. You say one o'clock that shit means three o'clock." One of the niggas who had introduced himself as Shaq laughed.

Kimya cut her eyes at him and reached for the J from one of the other dudes sitting in on the cipher. She inhaled the thick smoke, passed the J and walked into the engineering board. That shit shocked me because Kim looked like a fly girl – like she had no business fucking around with music. Shaq quickly followed her into the room that held the equipment and said, "Time to make magic."

I was in awe that she was going to run the boards. Dread brought me back from my thoughts.

"So, you couldn't have enjoyed the show that night I met you because after I got off the stage you were nowhere to be found." He said smiling and showing me all thirty-two of his pearly whites.

"Something came up." I stammered. I hear you had a good time anyway."

"You heard? What you hear about me?" He quizzed looking puzzled at my statement.

"You ended up having some groupie love with my best friend." I blurted out. Dread instantly turned red. He was obviously embarrassed by the situation.

"Wow! Now that's different. I guess the odds were against me. That shit just happened. I didn't go at her, she came at me." Dread said.

I looked at him with major attitude. No he didn't just sit there and try to go on about NiQue. I knew she was a roller, but he didn't have to put it out there like that.

"Look shawty no disrespect; it is what it is. It happened. It might not have happened if you hadn't rolled out."

I folded my arms and tried to ignore him. I focused on Nato laying down some mean lyrics. I understood why they called him God's Gift. He was nasty with his delivery and punch lines. Dread tried to capture my attention by passing me the J.

"Look shawty, you can sit there with your face balled up if you want. Shit happened, I wish it wouldn't have gone down like that, but I can't change it. You gonna' stay mad at me forever?"

He poked out his bottom lip and made a puppy dog face. He stuck out his hand as a gesture of a truce. I took his hand and shook it. We sat listening to some of the different members of The Cap lay down verses. I found talking to him was different from talking to dudes who didn't know anything but drugs, sex, and money. He was college educated, although he looked like he was a drug dealing thug. Nato had finished his recording and noticed that Dread and I had become quite friendly, and he didn't seem to mind. When he joined our conversation, Dread explained that we had met previously. I wasn't sure, but I don't think Nato gave a damn either way and he went in search of *Coronas*. Another group entered the studio and it was beginning to get crowded. It was starting to get late and I made my way out of the studio accompanied by Dread who insisted that he walk me out to my car.

"YaYa, I enjoyed chatting it up with you. Maybe we can do it again sometime."

"I would like that." I said writing my cell number on a flyer that I had taken off of my windshield.

He was standing next to my driver's side window, leaning his 6'3" frame partially inside. I couldn't help but want him. He was the complete package. He was fine, smart, and best of all…had no street dealings. Although we had spoken on many things, I did not discuss my line of work. Dread leaned in further and I could smell the scent of *Big Red* on his breath and he kissed my lips so tenderly that my body shook. I gathered what was left of my composure and pulled away from him thinking of NiQue. Even though she was going to use him for all she could and could care less about him, I felt guilty.

"Dread, I don't think we should go there. You gotta' understand that NiQue is my folks. She's like my sister, I guess you could say. I don't want to betray her trust." I said sliding my shades down over my eyes so he couldn't see that my eyes were saying, *I want you.*

"I hear you shawty." He said backing away from the car window.

Damn he was fine; from his long red locks, down to his *New Balance* clad feet. This man was on the money. I knew I had better pull off before I decided to say, *fuck NiQue!* I waved at him again and headed to Georgetown to get ready to live it up with NiQue at Ibiza. Once I reached my driveway, I saw NiQue's truck was there. I wondered how long she had been there. I walked into the house with my bags from earlier. "I'm home." I said entering the foyer. I was greeted by Oscar who was coming from Daddy's office which was right off the front door entrance.

"Oscar, how long has NiQue been here?" I questioned.

"She has been here for a few hours. She came in with her brother. He had some business with your father. Why?" He countered.

"Oh, I just wanted to know, I said continuing on to the family room where I found NiQue and Neko playing the *Wii.* They were deep into the game they were playing and hadn't noticed me enter the room. Neko was high as hell and NiQue was probably just as fucked up.

"Hey ya'll." I said letting them know I was there. They both jumped like they had heard the words, *this is a stick up.*

"Sup sis." Neko said turning to greet me.

"Imma' get up with you later on for that rematch." NiQue winked her eye at Neko. He blushed and turned back to the game.

I found that shit to be funny.

"We gonna' get this party started or what?" NiQue said brushing past me and heading to the stairs towards my room.

"Looks like you already started." I said

We were both getting ready for our night out and thoughts of Dread kept creeping into my mind. Damn, I hated when a nigga had me feeling all school girlish. NiQue was eyeing me while I stood naked in front of my full-length mirror applying apple-scented lotion to my juicy black skin. NiQue was pulling on the "loud" she had twisted up, and from the look in her eyes, she was rolling hard off of the X. I wasn't rolling, but I was high as hell, and we were sipping on some *Ciroc* so we would be nice and fucked up before we got to the club. I pulled on my teal bra and thong set from *Fredrick's of Hollywood* and slid into my little black dress that I had purchased earlier from the Solbiato shop. I made sure the holster containing my knife couldn't be detected.

NiQue was dressed and ready to party. She wore a blue fitted top with some bad ass black *Gucci* shorts that stopped right at the cuff of her fluffy ass. With some strappy *Gucci* shoes and bag to match, she was ready to stop traffic in her outfit. I stepped into my shoes and was ready to go out and let my hair down because I swear I needed to have a good time. Too much had happened and it was time for me to release some tension. We hopped in the back of the Escalade that was to be driven by Daddy's driver. We decided to have someone else drive us because we were far to fried to drive anywhere. We pulled in front of the club and walked right to the front of the line which was entirely too long. We flashed our boy, Brucie from Trinidad, a smile and he ushered us into the club.

It was good to know Brucie was doing well for himself and had landed himself a legal job. Brucie had been caught up on some murder beefs and somehow, anybody who had anything to do with the case turned up missing. After being held for a year and some change, Brucie was free to go. Since his release, he had been on the straight and narrow and wouldn't even think about illegal activity. It still amazed me that he could still live and work in the same city that had almost caused him to spend the rest of his life in jail or put him six feet deep!

We found ourselves being groped and fondled as we made our way through the hot club. The females all resembled Nicki Minaj with colorful hair and loud apparel. I guess Nicki was the "in" thing. The "Barbie" look was a bit much for my taste though. I swayed my hips to the beat while I walked to the bar to elevate my high. NiQue was right on my heels. We made it to the overcrowded bar and NiQue was trying to get the bartender's attention. Her cleavage was bursting out of her v-cut shirt and that made the bartender take notice.

He took our drink orders and NiQue gave him her credit card to start a tab. I was feeling real good and decided to go and find a boy toy for the night. NiQue and I made our way to the middle of the dance floor and started to dance. We were really having a good time when a light skinned brother with bad acne tried his hand. He was rubbing his hard, little dick all on my butt. I wasn't feeling it at all; mentally or physically. NiQue knew the look I was throwing her and quickly pulled me close to her and started grinding on me from the back.

NiQue shot the dude a look that said, *she's with me*, and home boy looked like he had just nutted in his pants. After a few more dances and plenty rounds of *Ciroc*, we were just about ready to leave. NiQue turned her attention to Sheik who was bunned up in a booth with his on again, off again, girlfriend Shawnna. I walked over to their table and greeted them. I kept it short and sweet since I knew there was no hope for me and him after she had flashed me a huge rock on her left hand. I told him I would get up with him on that business he was discussing with NiQue earlier, and then I made my exit.

The DJ was playing "No Hands" and I wanted Sheik to know exactly what he was going to be missing. I didn't give a fuck what Shawnna thought about it either. My dress had risen right to the cuff of my chocolate ass cheeks and I started making my ass clap to the beat. Shawnna just stared at me with looks that could kill. Sheik on the other hand couldn't stop watching me make my ass bounce to the beat of the music. NiQue knew exactly what I was doing and even though she was friends with Shawnna, I was her dog. She understood what I was doing. She told Shawnna she had to get my drunk ass home and we left. I could hear Shawnna screaming at Sheik for watching my porn show antics with so much lust. I felt satisfied that my work was done and we hopped in the Escalade just as the DJ said, "Last call for alcohol."

Once we got to my house, NiQue was still rolling off of the four pills she had taken through the course of the night. I was so gone off the drink and green that I was keyed up. I stood to remove my dress exposing my partially naked body to NiQue who was watching me lustfully. She stood and walked up behind me and ran her hands down the sides of my *Coke* bottle hips. I shuddered from her touch. Normally, I wouldn't even entertain the thought of NiQue touching me, but with all the shit going on, and my stress and frustration rising, allowed me to enjoy her touch. She turned me around to face her and she pulled me close to kiss her. I accepted her warm tongue and rubbed her huge ass; pulling her closer to me so that we were skin to skin. NiQue wiggled out of her shorts and pushed me backwards to the bed. She lay on top of me, kissing and sucking on my breasts.

"Sssssssss...YaYa, imma' make that pussy cum!" She said in between sucking on my nipples. Just the thought of her tasting my pussy made my pussy thump. No one had touched me in weeks, and I was due to cum and not by my own hands. I needed some maintenance and I didn't mind that it was coming from NiQue. She licked all over my stomach and moved down further still. Her head went down further, and she licked on my healthy thigh and parted my shivering legs. I was so wet with anticipation of feeling her suck on my clit. As if she knew what I was thinking, NiQue buried her face in my neatly waxed pussy. I was moaning and tossing and turning in no time. I was cumming over and over and NiQue showed no signs of stopping. She licked on my swollen clit like I was her lollipop. I thrust my hips upwards to her warm waiting mouth. I could feel my orgasm building as she continued to keep up with my rhythm. I was about to go over the edge when she slid her finger into my ass. It sent chills up my spine. I could hear the sounds of my wet pussy as she continued to finger fuck my ass and lick on my clit in a circular motion.

"Awwww…shit NiQue! You are gonna' make me cum!" I shouted while grinding my pussy all over her face. NiQue grabbed me by my soft ass and dug her nails into my cheeks raising my hips off of the bed.

"Fuck my mouth YaYa." She said between me humping and grinding on her face.

I couldn't take it anymore. I grabbed the back of her head and wound my wet pussy in her eager mouth and came. NiQue moved from between my legs with her face glistening like a glazed doughnut. She worked her way back up my body kissing me; allowing me to taste my own juices. NiQue had settled her middle over my leg and I could feel her wetness and it turned me on. She began to move up and down and back and forth on my thick thighs. I could feel how wet she was and wanted to help make her cum. She dismounted my legs and ordered me to turn over. I did as she said and she settled on top of my ass and began to ride until she yelped with pleasure. She grinded on me while she slid her slick fingers in and out of my moist pussy. I was rolling my hips around to meet her thrusts when she started to shake as she came all over my rotund booty.

NiQue climbed off of me panting, then rolled over on her side right behind me. I knew what we had done had crossed the line, but I didn't give a fuck because it felt great. I laid there feeling NiQue working her fingers in and out of my pussy until I came again and drifted off to sleep.

CHAPTER 17

420 Friendly Radio
Oxon Hill, MD

I woke the next morning to my cell phone vibrating across the dresser. I looked for NiQue, but she obviously had left. I rolled out of the bed and grabbed my phone. I had missed three messages. One of the messages came from Corrine informing me that she needed to hook up with me. I knew that was a money move. The next message was from NiQue that simply said, "Our lil' secret." I erased that message and tried to shake what had happened the night before from my mind. I knew a line had been crossed. The last message was from an unknown number. It just stated that I needed to call the number back. My head was throbbing slightly from the *Ciroc*, so I knew it was going to be a long day. I waited on calling the number back. I showered, dressed, and made my way down the hall towards the staircase when I saw that Neko's door was ajar, and he was in his room alone for once. Curious to what was going on with him, I pushed the door open further and walked in.

"Damn you don't knock no more shawty?" Neko said, grinning when he saw me.

I flopped on the bed and just stared at my brother like he was an alien. He had changed so much since the first day I had met him. He had grown a few inches taller, and I could tell he had much more bass in his voice from when he first moved in. He was becoming a man. Worse than that, he had a taste for the street life and it wouldn't let him go.

"What's your plan for the day? Which chick you hooking up with?" I asked.

"Damn, nobody! I was gonna probably hit the mall with NiQue. She said she wanted to find some new shoes. I saw some fly ass *Jordans* that I got to get. Neko said.

"Since when did you and NiQue get so close that you are hanging and shopping and shit?"

"Ain't she like family to you? Why can't she be like family to me?" I thought about it and felt guilty. I felt guilty for half ass accusing my brother of sleeping with my best friend who I had fucked the night before. "I ain't tripping; she is family. I was just wondering how you got to be so close. I barely see her these days." I said trying to play it off.

"Naw, she come by every now and again. We smoke and talk." He said.

"Have you seen Daddy? I saw him last week and then that was it." I asked him.

"He and Oscar have been hanging real close. They have been talking about a lot of business and how Pops got some trouble with some folks." He said nonchalantly. My heart started pounding and I could feel my palms getting clammy. It felt like someone had cut off my air supply.

"So, when was someone going to tell me some shit was happening? What kind of trouble? Trouble with who? Why hasn't anybody said anything to me?" I asked.

"I got this around here!" Neko said.

He lifted the plain white tee he was wearing and exposed the butt of a gun. I couldn't tell what kind it was, and it didn't matter either.

"What the fuck are you doing with that?"

He let his shirt fall back over his waistband and walked to me.

"YaYa, it's real out here. Pops got some shit going on and he ain't talking about it. You know he ain't going to tell me anyway. You're running around here smoking niggas in parking garages and you bugging because I got a pistol? Come on! Get the fuck out of here with that! I mean you really thought I was going to sit around and wait for niggas to come for one of ya'll without going out without a fight?" He shook his head and stopped moving towards me. "Look, YaYa you ain't the only one around here that can put a nigga on his back. All I am saying is, I got it for protection." He explained.

I didn't even want to hear any more. I just wanted to go and make arrangements for my brother and father to leave the area. I started to walk out of Neko's room without saying a word about what I was doing or where I was going. I turned to face him and simply told him to pack his shit because we were going to be gone by morning. He didn't say a word back. He just looked at me like he wasn't really trying to hear what I was saying. He didn't know I would force his ass out by gunpoint if I had to.

I walked out and slammed the door behind me. He was out of his mind if he thought I was going to sit around and just wait for some shit to pop off and not try to avoid it. I went down the stairs to Daddy's office. I walked straight in without knocking, and as usual, no one was there. Not Oscar or Daddy. I kept it moving and headed out the house to Corrine since she had some money for me. I was sure I was going to need it because as far as I was concerned, we were leaving in the morning! I remembered the message that said to call them and decided I should do just that. I dialed the number and the phone was answered by a gruff voice.

"Cap Citi Studios, you got Butta."

"Well, Butta is it?" I asked. "Did someone call YaYa?"

I heard him ask the voices in the background did someone call me. I heard some more shuffling and then Dread came on the line. "Damn girl, took you long enough to call me back." He joked.

"I have a lot going on, plus I don't answer numbers I don't know on this phone." I said giving up much attitude.

"Well, I am glad you called me back. You busy today? I have a show and I would love for you to come."

"I have some stuff brewing with my family, but I am sure I could make some time to see your performance."

He gave me the address to the venue and hung up. I pulled out of the driveway headed into the city to Southeast to collect my money.

Chapter 18

The Goodman/Barry Farms
SE Washington, DC

I had made my way to Southeast in under fifteen minutes, which had to be some kind of world record. You can't get anywhere in DC in fifteen minutes, yet, somehow I did. Traffic was always a nightmare and not to mention the one-way streets that confuse even the most seasoned driver. Although the Nation's Capital is only a hole in the ground, no bigger than four or five miles, I am sure I haven't seen all of it yet. I stepped out of the car and entered Corrine's building. When I reached her floor, I noticed her front door was ajar.

I hesitated because Corrine was very cautious and played by the rules. She would never just leave her shit open. She lived in the heart of the hood. Southeast is the Devil's Playground. No one was safe. A Preacher ain't safe in his own church on Easter in the DMV. A nigga was always on the prowl for a come up, what a thirsty nigga would need to hit pay dirt was an open door. I hated to do it in her pissy hallways, but I removed my heels and stuck them in my purse. I exchanged my shoes for Chase. My heart was pounding and I was sure the whole hood could hear it thumping in my chest. I pushed the door open further as quietly as I could. I walked in to what appeared to be an empty apartment. Amazingly, all of Corrine's stuff was still there. I pushed the door closed behind me. I could feel my heartbeat slow down and my breathing return to its normal rhythmic pace.

I guess the silly bitch left out and didn't close it all the way. It's a wonder she hadn't been robbed blind. I sat my purse down on the coffee table and made my way to the back of the apartment. The hair on the back of my neck stood up and sent off alarms that something wasn't right. I still had Chase in my hands because I swore I would never be caught without her again. Something told me even though shit looked sweet, it looked too sweet. I entered the first bedroom and everything looked ok. I backed out of that room and headed where Corrine's office was. That door was open and I could see a clear view of the desk. I inched up the hallway and entered the room. Everything seemed like it was in order, until I looked at the closet door which looked like it had been kicked in. I tip toed over to the closet and peeked inside.

It took everything in me not to scream from the horror show inside. Corrine was shot in the head. She was just laying there with a blank stare on her face. She looked as if she knew the end was coming and there was no way to stop it. Somehow, whoever got in had managed to hit Corrine and two bitches she had in the apartment with her. I could feel the bile building in my throat looking at their bodies shoved into that small space. Each girl had been shot with no regard. I could not believe what I had just walked into. I turned to leave when I saw one sheet of paper on the desk. Damn near running over to the desk, I snatched up the piece of paper. It simply read, "YaYa, we got you next."

I turned and walked quickly and as quietly as I had come, taking the paper with me. Tears were streaming down my face and I was fueled by fear. I was able to compose myself long enough to grab my purse up off of the table and leave Corrine's tomb. As soon as I got out of those pissy hallways and got to the safety of my car, I threw up. I sat there in a daze for several minutes before I collected myself enough to drive. I pulled away from the curb and headed to Cap Citi Studios. I don't know what made me go there, but it was closer than going home in case someone had seen me. Someone had definitely meant for me to get the message. Someone was gunning for me, and I had no idea who it was. Someone had been causing problems for Daddy, and now someone was after me. The day had started out fucked up, and it seemed as if it was going to get much worse. I called Dread on the number he had given me as his cell because I sure wasn't going to call the studio. I don't know what made me trust him, but at that point there was no one else to call close by. I silently prayed that he would answer. After the third ring, I was expecting an automated voice to tell me to leave a message.

"Wassup shawty?" He answered. Thank God he answered.

"Can I meet up with you somewhere? I know you have a show tonight, but I need somewhere to get my mind right for a second. You are still on the Southside; right?

"Yeah, what's going on? You aight?" He asked concerned.

"Yes, I'll explain when I get there." I answered.

After he gave me the address, I started in the direction of the address. When I pulled up, I noticed Dread was out front with some youngins. I found a parking space and shut down the engine of the car. Before stepping out, I surveyed my surroundings. The neighborhood he had led me to wasn't the safest. The parking lot was straight out of a bad nightmare. Although my whole life was dedicated to creating neighborhoods like the one I was looking at, I still couldn't get used to fucked up hood living. There were people all over the place. Mainly niggas looking to get high or niggas trying to get money. Either way, I wasn't sure if I wanted to leave the safety of my car. While I was contemplating just driving off, Dread tapped on the window. I almost jumped out of my skin.

"Are you just gonna' sit in the car, or are you gonna get out and tell me to what I owe the honor?"

I grabbed my bag because Chase was chilling in the bottom and I wasn't about to go anywhere without her. I opened my door and checked out my surroundings and decided that if someone was gonna get me they certainly weren't going to do it in broad daylight where there were about fifty people milling around. But then again, when shit went down in the hood, ain't nobody see shit. That was bonafide hood rules. You either lived by them or died by them. Once I got out, Dread led me down a long walk way that ended in a courtyard with a cluster of apartments towering over it. We got to a security door that was anything but secure. We walked in and up to the third floor. When he opened his apartment door, it was a typical male's home. It was neat, but you could tell when a woman wasn't in the equation. For some reason, that made me feel relieved. I found a seat near the window so I could keep an eye on my car and anyone who got near it.

"You aight over there? You sounded like you had some serious shit going on. You almost made me afraid to give you the address." He chuckled.

"You got a roll up?" I asked after digging in my bag and retrieving some of the Loud I had in my Louie.

I guess he was shocked to see a chick that came prepared. If me smoking was shocking, then what would he do if he found out why I really came to his house? He passed me a cigarillo and just stared at me like he was trying to put together the pieces of a puzzle. After what felt like forever, he spoke.

"So what brought you to me today? I would have thought you were out shopping for tonight or going to get your nails done. You know some girly stuff."

"Nah. I have to be honest with you. I don't know why I am here. I went to see some folks and I found them murked in the closet of their apartment." I continued to break down the weed and avoid whatever expression Dread had on his face.

"Damn shawty. Someone had it out for them folks; huh? You ain't think to call the Feds? You just left them in the closet? That's some gangster shit!" I was beginning to regret ever opening my mouth.

"There are a lot of things you don't know about me." I said trying to shut him up.

"Then humor me and tell me, because you already got a nigga's head spinning."

"Look, I found out this morning someone has some stuff stirred up with my Dad. My little brother is out of control, and then my visit to my girl's house and finding her like that. This day is a do over. I want to go back to last night and do this shit differently. You just don't know the half."

I had tears seeping from my eyes. I hadn't even noticed I had been crying. Too many emotions had consumed me all at once. Dread took the weed and finished twisting up while I cried. I cried over all the confusion going on. I sat there smoking with Dread and he tried to get me to talk. Not about the events of the day, but about me.

"So, what does YaYa do?" He asked.

"I thought you already knew what YaYa did. She shops and gets her nails done." I laughed. "I am really a Daddy's girl at heart. He has always taken care of me. Whatever I wanted he got it for me."

"Oh, so you a brat huh?" Hey what is your real name? I am sure your Momma and Daddy ain't name you YaYa.

"No smart ass, they didn't name me YaYa. My father calls me YaYa. My name is YaSheema, since you have to know." I answered.

I looked at him and could tell there was so much tension in

the room you could feel it crawling down the walls and oozing through the noisy heating and cooling unit. It was like we were both searching for something to say other than the obvious. Both of us knew we had no business wanting or desiring the other. I can't explain it, but I felt safe with him. I felt like I could tell him all my secrets and they would be safe. He was the comfort of an old friend.

"I ain't never heard the name YaSheema before. That sounds like the name of a chick who's daddy owns a carry-out and Papa Son got caught playing in chocolate." He laughed snapping me out of my thoughts.

"You better be glad I have heard that shit so much growing up that it ain't even funny anymore. Everyone has a name joke."

"I didn't mean to offend you Ms. YaSheema."

"No offense taken."

"Good, because I would hate to upset you."

He got up and moved over to where I was sitting, and made himself comfortable next to me. I felt uneasy with him being so close to me. He tapped my thigh to pass me the J. I took a deep long pull and tried to sort out the details of the day. I had gone to bed with some bullshit brewing, woke up to some bullshit brewing, and was continuing into my day with a cup that runneth over with shit. The longer I sat trying to make sense of it all, the more aggravated I became. I knew I had better get out of there before I did something else that I would regret. Just as I was thinking about how I was going to leave, my cell phone began to vibrate in my purse signaling a text message.

Breaking the uncomfortable silence, I dug around in my bag to find my phone. I unlocked the screen and it was a message from Neko. It was only one word, but it was menacing all the same. It was the scariest three-lettered word I had ever had the misfortune of reading. It read, "RUN." Quickly rising to my feet and startling

Dread, I dropped the J in the ashtray and grabbed my purse from where it was resting.

"I gotta' go. There is something going on with my little brother." I stammered.

"Is everything ok?" Dread asked looking worried.

"It will be." I responded as I made my way out the door. I wasn't sure about what I just said about it being ok. Nothing in the whole day had gone right.

I don't know why I hadn't done what Neko had instructed me to do. Instead, I hopped in my ride and started for Georgetown. Doing way past the legal speed limit, I hit the highway and floored the gas. I couldn't think straight. I knew it was nothing but trouble because Neko had just told me to run after basically telling me he would do no such thing. I was trying my best to keep calm and focus on getting home. Finally hitting Georgetown, I turned on Wisconsin Avenue unaware of the company I had following me a few car lengths behind.

Pulling into the driveway, nothing seemed out of order. Daddy's truck was in the garage, and the door was open. Daddy did that from time to time when he intended to leave right out. I suspected that maybe he, Neko and Oscar were on their way out of the house. Barely putting the car in park, and snatching the keys from the ignition, I pushed open my door and rushed up the drive and into the garage bay. I noticed the door leading to the house from the garage was ajar. Pushing the door open and trying to enter, the door stopped. There was something blocking it from opening all the way. I put some force behind it and pushed the door and heard a loud groan coming from the other side. The grunting sound caused me step back from the entry way.

"Get help." Oscar gurgled from the other side of the door.

I could hear the urgency in his voice, and it was unlike anything I had ever heard from him before. It made me force myself to react.

I ran out of the garage as fast as my feet would carry me and made my way to the front door. I was doing too many things all at once. I was fumbling for the keys and calling 911. The dispatcher came on the line asking me to state the nature of my emergency.

"My uncle is hurt." I whispered into the receiver, not knowing if someone was still lurking around inside the house just waiting on me. I gave the operator the address and disconnected the call.

It was the second time that day that I had walked into some shit. Entering the foyer, I wasn't prepared for what came next. All of the artwork that normally neatly lined the walls of the hallway were laying scattered about the foyer floor. I crept as quietly as I could in the direction of the garage and stopped in my tracks. I could hear death ringing in my ears. I was torn between tending to Oscar, finding Neko and finding Daddy. I figured I would go to Oscar and he would tell me where to find Daddy and Neko. I headed to the garage and I could hear my heart pounding in my chest. It sounded just like a college drum line. I walked down the hallway and past the dining area. That's where I found him. I screamed. I screamed a gut wrenching scream. A scream so sickening that it would rock one's entire being.

My father was lying in a pool of blood with gunshot wounds to his upper torso. He lay there lifeless and cold. I ran to him and slipped in the pool of blood surrounding him. I gathered myself as much as one could in a situation like that, and crawled the rest of the distance to my father's body. I scooped him into my arms and cried. I cried for what felt like hours. I held him and shook him not wanting the shit to be really be happening to me. I forgot about Neko. I forgot about Oscar too. It was like time stood still and nothing else seemed to exist. I shook Daddy. I had tears streaming down my cheeks. I felt a piece of me dying. I knew my father was dead; but I refused to leave him there to find out if Neko was dead too. My life flashed before me. I started seeing past birthdays, and happy moments of my life that Daddy made special for me. The police found me right in that spot, hugging and rocking Daddy as if he were a baby.

They immediately started asking me questions about anyone else being in the house. I listened as more sirens wailed in the distance. I nodded and pointed to the garage which was off to the right of where I was sitting with Daddy in my arms. I looked down at my father's face and squeezed my eyes real tight and I swore I heard him talking to me. I heard Daddy call my name.

"YaYa, you have got to toughen up. Now is not the time to fall apart. Get your shit together!"

When I opened my eyes, the rest of the police I had heard in the distance, had entered the house and must have thought I was in complete shock. They tried their best to separate me from Daddy's body and I wasn't having it without a fight. I totally flipped out when they pronounced him dead. I became enraged and tried to attack anyone who got near him. I was kicking and screaming while they were toe tagging Daddy's body and in walked Detective Gatsby. He was the last person I wanted to see. From the search of the house that was conducted there was no sign of Neko. I didn't know if that was a good or bad thing. Someone had stolen my entire world from me and that shit hurt. I didn't give a fuck about too many people in life, but my father and my brother were definitely the two I cared about the most. Now Daddy was dead and Neko was missing.

Oscar was rushed to the hospital with gunshot wounds right under his collar bone and in his leg. He had lost so much blood they weren't sure if he was going to make it. Yeah, shit was fucked up. Then I had that detective on my ass again. Death was following me and it wasn't hard to tell. I thought I had tied up any loose ends from Papi, so I had no idea why someone wanted me dead. It was the kind of shit you saw on the news and prayed it never happened to anyone you loved. Gatsby questioned the first officers to respond to the call and they had told him what they had found up to that moment, which hadn't been too much.

CHAPTER 19

Gatsby followed YaSheema since earlier that day and lost her somewhere in the congestion of Georgetown traffic. Nothing had seemed abnormal in her travels. She had ventured to Southeast DC and made two stops since leaving her home. She had gone to a well-known drug area known as the Parklands. She had entered one of the buildings and left after about ten minutes or so. From there she had driven to a different section of Southeast and was met by an unknown black male whom she accompanied into another apartment building.

Gatsby hadn't thought much of her travels until she had rushed out of the building about an hour or so later in a big hurry. She had a look of worry on her face. She got in her car and broke all types of laws and speed limits from one side of the city to the other. Gatsby hadn't tried to stop her or detain her so he could see if he could find out what had her shook up. Somewhere on M Street, Gatsby had lost her and figured she was heading home.

Unfortunately, YaSheema had come home to a grizzly scene.

Her father had been brutally murdered in his home and long-time family friend, Oscar Jones had been critically wounded and was fighting for his life in a nearby hospital. Once the officers were able to get YaSheema out of the house and to the station, she wouldn't talk.

Gatsby knew she knew more than she was letting on, but she wouldn't open her mouth about it. Something, or someone, had led her home. The call for distress didn't come over the police radio until after he had followed her good into Georgetown and lost her. So far, the girl had witnessed her boyfriend murdered, and then someone tried to wipe out her entire family. Gatsby had no idea how he was going to get her to talk, but he had to try. He tried to make sense of all of the senseless violence that seemed to be following YaSheema and could not make heads or tails of any of it. No one should have that much bad luck. Gatsby had covered all of his bases before even trying to question her. His questioning of the girl's "so called" uncle was useless. He had been Medevac'd out to Prince Georges Hospital Center. He said the same thing the police already knew. Nothing.

He said he had been preparing to escort Mr. Clayton out on some random errands and was met in the garage by masked individuals. That was all he could provide. Gatsby popped open his bottle of antacids. He shook three out of their container and ate all of them and washed them down with a warm *Pepsi*. Gatsby pushed the pencil round and round his desk before pushing his roll chair away from his desk and standing up. Hating to be the one to have to question the girl again; Gatsby prepared himself for what he knew was going to be damn near impossible. Getting anything out of the daughter of the late, kingpin, Darnell S. Clayton would take a miracle. She had already proved to be a hard ass.

Walking out of his office and into the questioning room, he turned the knob to find YaSheema sitting with a blank stare on her beautiful ebony face. She looked as though her soul was lost. The shit that happened to her was worse for her than the hit on her boyfriend. She had all the classic signs of shock starting to set in, and Gatsby wondered if he should get her some medical attention.

As if she were reading his mind, YaYa spoke up. "No, I am not crazy yet; but if you all don't find out who did this to my family someone else may need medical attention. I am in no mood for playing games with you or anyone else. Detective Gatsby, let's get this straight right now. I don't know what happened. I don't know who would want to hurt my Dad and Oscar. I received a text message from my brother who told me to "run." Instead of running, I went straight home and found Oscar and Daddy like that. I cannot find my baby brother and I am afraid for his life." YaSheema had decided to tell Gatsby about her brother just as a pre-caution.

"YaSheema, as I promised you before, I will find out what happened to your loved ones. Do you think any of this was connected with the murder of your boyfriend?" He asked as gingerly as he could. He didn't want to set her off again.

I cringed and shifted in my seat at the mention of Papi. I had handled all loose ends dealing with him, unlike the stupid detective who was still looking for his killer whom he would never find because I had deaded that bitch days ago!

"Detective to be honest with you, it could have been anyone."

"YaSheema, do you know where your brother could have gone if he indeed made it out of the house before the violence occurred? He could be the missing piece to this puzzle."

I cocked my head to the side as if I were in deep thought. I knew where he was, but I wasn't going to tell the Feds anything before I got a chance to talk to him. I was willing to bet my left hand to God that he had made his way to Trinidad to NiQue's. Where else was he to go?

"No detective, I don't know where he could be. Please find him because he is all I have left in this world besides Oscar, and I am not going to sit here and wait for some more bad news." I demanded.

I thought by adding that would convince the nosey ass detective that I didn't know anything in regards to my brother's location.

"Ahhh…Ms. Clayton, may I ask where your mother is? I have her listed as Christa Reynolds. Maybe your brother went to her for help."

I shook my head. "My mother left my father's home months ago and hasn't been seen since. You see my brother is my half brother. He was not my father's son. My mother came back into my life about seven months ago and then she disappeared and left Neko with us. My Dad took on the role of being Neko's provider. We have no idea where Christa is." I stated coldly.

My cell phone began to vibrate. It stopped Gatsby from moving to his next question about where he could possibly look to find Christa. The text read, "Call me when they let you go." It was Neko. I could feel the headache I had acquired starting to subside with just that text. I knew he was safe and that made me feel much better than I had felt all day.

After receiving that text from Neko, I was able to breeze through the rest of the questions with ease. Once Gatsby was finished playing twenty questions with me, I gathered my things and left the station. I hadn't even noticed that I was still wearing the blood stained clothing from holding my father in my arms. I damn near ran to my car and jumped inside and began dialing NiQue's number because I dared not call Neko on his phone because that retarded cop had made it seem that Neko may have had something to do with all of the shit going down, and I sure didn't want Neko involved in my mess any further than he already was. NiQue answered on the first ring. I wasn't going to talk too much.

"Aye NiQue, is he there?" I asked.

"Yes, he is here. Are you ok? Do you need me to come and get you? Where are you? What happened?"

I wasn't feeling her. She should have known better than to ask me a bunch of questions. She was starting to get on my nerves here lately. I wasn't going to answer shit and she had Neko right there with her. I am sure he could answer all of the questions she had. I pressed the end button on the phone and tossed it to the passenger seat. I drove in the direction of Northeast DC.

I slid in a Cap Citi/Kushboys CD and needed some motivation to stay strong and to ride the shit out until the wheels fell off. "I'm A Winner" by Lucky Lamar and Mama's Moonshine came pouring through the *Bose* system. They were singing the truth. I was a winner but I was losing so much, so fast; it was hard to believe what had happened. I didn't even want to think about my Daddy not being around with me. As far as I was concerned, he was right there with me. I puffed on a Djarum as I sped through the busy streets of Drama City. I reached NiQue's house and Neko was sitting on her front porch. His eyes were red and all of NiQue's father's guards were posted all around. You would think they were just niggas hanging out if you didn't know any better. I ran full speed to my brother's waiting arms. I could tell he had been crying and he wasn't hiding how hurt he was with what had happened. He loved Daddy just as much as I had because he was one of the only people who loved him as much as I did.

Neko pulled me into his embrace and cried.

"Neko what happened?" I asked confused. "I went to make a run to Corrine's house and found her folded up in the closet. Neko, I ran from there to Dread's house and that's when I got your text." I continued. I was just spilling my guts and not even paying attention to NiQue who was taking in every word. I saw how she had grimaced when I mentioned Dread. She would have to get over that shit and understand that he and I were just friends. Although I didn't owe her any explanations, I felt like that needed to be explained, but it just wasn't the time. I had more important shit on my mind. I held on to Neko tight and cried. I held him so tight because I felt like if I were to let him go, something bad would happen and I couldn't afford that. I searched all over his frame to make sure he was unharmed and continued.

"I came straight home as soon as I got your text. When I got there Oscar was hurt critically and Daddy is dead."

I began to tear up again and I felt faint. NiQue rushed over to my side and passed me a bottle of water. I tried to gather my composure so I could get Neko's take on the whole thing.

"Neko." I said between sniffles. "How did you get out of there? What happened in there?" I asked.

Neko was barely audible as he tried to run back the deadly events. He had tears soaking his face and was shaking so bad, he couldn't control it.

"I was about to leave to head over to this side of town and I went to ask Oscar to move Pop's car so I could get out of the drive way. When I came back to the garage, I saw the garage door was opened so I figured Oscar had moved the car. When I stepped into the garage from the house I saw Oscar running back into the car bay from the driveway. There was a dark colored van in the turn around and I knew who ever it was, wasn't invited. Something deep inside told me to go back inside the house. I ran. I ran up the stairs past my room and into Pop's room. I hid in the hide-a-way space in his closet. That's when I heard the shots fired. YaYa, I thought the gunshots would never stop. I sent you the text from Pop's closet. When the gun fire ceased I left out of the closet and ran out of the front door. I never looked back." Neko's voice had trailed off.

The tears were streaming from Neko's gray eyes. I don't know what was more heartbreaking. Losing my Daddy, or watching my brother, who was such a warrior earlier, cry like a baby. I felt woozy listening to Neko relive the whole ordeal. NiQue was crying as if she had lost one of her own. Something inside of me clicked and I stopped crying. I wiped away the tears and stood up. I still wasn't sure if I was strong enough to stand and walk on my own, but I was going to try.

"NiQue, I have some things I have to handle and since my home is a crime scene and Neko and I cannot just walk back in there safely, can he stay here?" I asked.

NiQue nodded her head up and down slowly. I couldn't quite read her emotions. She looked like she felt sorry for us. She had a look of sadness in her eyes, but there was something sinister lurking behind the sadness. She wasn't happy about the Dread comment, and I knew we were going to have to talk about that shit at some point. I, on the other hand, was on a mission to find out who had set out to destroy me and my family. I started walking down the sidewalk towards my car that was parked haphazardly at the curb, and Neko ran up behind me.

"YaYa, I am coming with you. You ain't leaving me here while you out there." He said wiping away his tears.

I looked at my baby brother and had to remind myself he was raised to try and take care of shit no matter how bad it was. He may have looked like a grown man, but he wasn't ready for all that was going on. There was no way I was dragging him into that shit.

"Neko, I have to find out who did this to us and you cannot get yourself involved. It seems as though whoever is after the family doesn't know about you, and I want to keep it that way."

Neko opened his mouth to argue, but I stopped him before he could even formulate the words to try and convince me that riding out with me was the smart thing to do. I didn't want to leave him because I didn't know if I was ever going to see him again, but I couldn't risk him getting hurt or even worse, killed…because of me. Maybe he knew that coming with me wasn't a good idea, because he didn't ask or try to join me again. NiQue just nodded her head at me as if to say she knew her position and she was going to look after my baby brother. I got in the car and pulled away from the curb with my baby brother and best friend watching me drive away to my unknown future.

CHAPTER 20

Marygold's Hall and Nightclub
Lanham, MD

I sat up in the bed looking out of my hotel window thinking to myself; my father was gone, and I couldn't make contact with my brother unless I wanted to put him in harm's way. NiQue seemed like she had a chip on her shoulder since she had heard me mention Dread's name. Oscar was in PG Hospital and from what the doctors were willing to tell me, being that I had no blood relation to him, he was stabilized but was still in serious condition. I had taken up temporary residence in the Hilton in Crystal City because I felt like it was safe to stay there. I had requested that several of NiQue's father's guards post up in and around the hotel. I had been there for four days. I had barely eaten, and I wasn't going to leave until I had a game plan.

Unfortunately for me, the streets weren't talking and that was a rarity. No one knew what the fuck was going on and that was driving me crazy. I was lucky that my father had employed loyal folks who would ride or die for us all. They were still putting in that work while I was free to grieve. The only person I had made contact with in regards to business was Caesar. I had to prove to him that it was still business as usual, and that the money was to keep flowing. I had to keep his greasy ass on my radar, because for all I knew, he could have been the one who had ordered the hit on my family. It was so strange that I was in charge of everything on my own. It was easy dealing with business. What was hard was dealing with burying my Daddy.

I decided to have the funeral even though the police suggested that we shouldn't have it in the area being that the crime was so horrific and they didn't know if whoever got Daddy would get me next. I thought they were crazy for even suggesting that my Daddy be buried somewhere else. He loved the city. He loved it for everything the place had to offer and everything it had become. I knew the police didn't really give a fuck what had happened to him. The only ones who cared were the ones that Daddy employed. I had already sent word through Epps, who was second in command under Oscar, that it was still as it had been before the untimely passing of my father.

I buried my Daddy on a Wednesday afternoon. I asked anyone that was attending to please wear white because black and dark colors were too damn depressing. The limo was to pick me up from the hotel I had been living in for the past week in under an hour, and I had not even begun to motivate myself to move from the safety of the hotel room. I didn't think I was going to be able to. The day had come too fast, and I kept telling myself that I was going to be strong. I kept hearing Daddy's voice telling me to *toughen up*.

I swung my legs over the side of the bed and stood. I felt the plush carpet between my toes – not wanting to leave the sanctuary of the hotel. I showered and got dressed in my peach-colored suit. I had asked everyone else to wear white and the family was to wear pastel colors. I did this for more than one reason. I needed to be able to identify everyone. Only friends knew to wear white, family knew to wear pastels. If you were wearing black or dark colors, my security team was going to keep an eye on you closely. I could not take any chances.

After looking myself over, I pulled on a pair of shades. No sooner than I had pulled them down over my eyes, I got a knock on the suite door. I peered out of the peephole to see Epps on the other side of the door and quickly opened it to let him know I was ready. I grabbed my handbag and walked back to the door to step into the hallway where the elevator was. In the hallway there were two other armed bodyguards posted up on the ends of the hall.

"Ms. Clayton, we have already picked up your brother and he is waiting in the limo." Epps said dryly. I nodded my head to acknowledge that I had heard him and stepped into the elevator. Once we reached the lobby, Epps stepped out in front of me before signaling me to exit.

Escorted by Epps, we walked out of the lobby and to the limo where Neko was dressed in a white *Hugo Boss* suit with a lavender shirt on under it and a white *Hugo Boss* tie. He looked like he was struggling with coping with the loss of Daddy too. I couldn't imagine how he was feeling. First Mommy's disappearance, and then Daddy's untimely death. He had to be torn up at all the loss he suffered. As soon as the limo door closed we embraced.

"YaYa, I can't stay cooped up at NiQue'shouse for too much longer. I am starting to go crazy just sitting in there doing nothing. I want to go home YaYa."

"Neko, I haven't even been home yet. Anything I needed from the house Epps has gotten for me," I said.

"Well, at least let me come and stay where ever it is you have been. I cannot do this without at least having you close by." He said trying to get me to break down. Honestly it wasn't hard to have us both posted up in the hotel and secured by Epps and his team. It may have proved to be easier than having us separated, but now was not the time to even worry about all of that. The ride to the funeral home was in silence. Neko and I exchanged glances, but no words. When we pulled up there was a sea of people wearing white on white out of respect. I took a deep breath grabbed Neko's hand and exited into the afternoon sunshine. I was more than thankful for the invention of sunglasses because as soon as we entered the funeral home and approached Daddy's casket, the tears began to pour freely.

I took steps slowly up the aisle and what I had been dreading become reality. My Daddy was laying there dead. All the money in the world could not bring him back to me, but he looked peaceful in his white, velvet-lined casket. Daddy's casket had the Lord's Prayers etched into the head of the casket so he could forever be in peace. The trim was laid in platinum and the assortment of carnations and roses lining the entire funeral home were beautiful. The amethyst and ruby spray with a rosary of roses that lined the inside of the casket were breath taking. It was such a shame that something so beautiful was going back to where it came, but not as gracefully as it had come. Into the earth.

I stood over top of my father's casket wondering how it had come to this. He had a slight smirk on his face, like he knew a secret and was not in the business of sharing it. I kissed his face and felt the coldness of his lifeless body against my lips and pulled away from the casket because I was becoming too overwhelmed with emotions. I took a few steps back and Neko held on to me for support. He took a few steps up to the casket and said his own goodbyes. You would have never known that Darnell Clayton and Neko Reynolds had no blood relation. Neko was heartbroken and crying. I slid my arm around his shoulders and we embraced for everyone to see. I cupped his chin in my hand and wiped away his tears. We finally started to make our way to the pews. I stopped dead in my tracks when I saw NiQue and her brother in the front row accompanied by Dread, Crack, Queen, Shaq, Kimya and NATO who were seated a row behind them.

Seeing Dread there surprised me being that I didn't know if he was there for me or for NiQue. I made my way to my seat and avoided making any eye contact with him. During the service I could feel him watching me and I wanted so desperately to talk to him and see what he knew about what was going on. Just because I didn't want NiQue to know how deep my friendship was with him, I refrained from making any eye contact with him at all.

The service was nice. Well...as nice as a home going could be. The preacher, who had never met my father, said so many wonderful things about him that you would have thought they were old friends. He only spoke on the good things we had told him my father had done for the community such as providing the funds for the new Boys and Girls Club to be constructed and the soup kitchen he donated thousands of dollars to each year. Not one word was spoken about his profession as a bonafide gangster and drug lord.

After the services were over, we were escorted out by our security detail and into the waiting limo. The pall bearers, dressed in white with white kid gloves, walked my father's body out into the waiting hearse. Daddy's body was then taken back to the hood where he grew up. He was to be buried in Mount Olivet in Trinidad Northeast. I watched them take my father's body from the hearse and place him over his open grave. Daddy was to be lowered into his grave while we were there. I wanted to leave nothing to chance. We exited the limo, and seated right in front of the casket followed by friends and family. That's when I noticed them. There were several men dressed in black that stood far off enough that they wouldn't be noticed, but close enough to tell that they were there for someone in our funeral party.

I started feeling my heart beat quicken. I knew something with those niggas wasn't quite right. First, they were dressed in the wrong color to be a part of Daddy's home going and secondly, I didn't recognize any of them. Epps must have sensed there was something wrong because he instantly got on point. He made eye contact with the rest of the goons we employed, and they started to move towards the uninvited guests. Right before they got close enough to the strangers, I saw the men dressed in black pull out high powered machine guns. I froze in place. Fear took over my body and I couldn't move from the place I was seated. Epps saw everything unfolding and pushed me and Neko to the ground.

There was madness unfolding all around us as the men dressed in black opened fire in my direction. I struggled to see what was happening as I was then rolled into my father's open grave by Epps. From the pit of the open grave I could hear all of the screams and running of all of the people attending the funeral. I didn't want to move. I couldn't move. I just waited. I could hear babies crying and women screaming. I could hear the gunfire ripping through flesh. I could smell the very familiar scent of gun powder and hot flesh wounds. As much as I thought I was a bred killer, I could never get used to the sounds of death. Bodies dropping, and the gurgling of a wounded bystander fighting as they take their last breath, was something I could never get used to.

When it seemed as though the hail of gunfire finally ceased, I took a deep breath. I could smell nothing but the cool earth that I had been forced into. I had remained still for what seemed like hours. I silently prayed that my friends and family were ok. Just as I was about to move to see if it was safe for me to call out for help, I saw Neko's face over the side of the open grave.

"YaYa, are you aight?" He almost whispered. I knew we weren't out of immediate danger just by the sound of his voice.

Next to him appeared Epps and the funeral director. They were lowering down jumper cables to help get me out of my father's tomb. I jumped for the cables when they were within my reach and dug my feet into the sides of the enclosure. Once I was pulled free from my father's grave, I lay there. I lay there on the side of the opening and just stared at the madness that had unfolded. My father's casket was turned over and there were bodies of members of the funeral party sprawled around.

I was brought out of my semi-trance by Neko who pulled me up to my feet and Dread had grabbed me around my waist, guiding me to the limo that had been driven over to the side of the grave to act as a shield. I got in and I vowed I would never be the same as we sped away. I knew there was a war brewing; but the question was, who was I battling?

CHAPTER 21

Upscale Ballroom
Suitland Road
Suitland, MD

O nce we arrived back at my hotel, I let Epps know I would
be fine. I stepped into the suite and took off my suit
jacket. I was startled by who was staring at me in the mirror. I was
a mess. I had dirt caked all over my face, and my peach dress was
stained from the grass and dirt from my roll into the grave.

I walked into the bathroom and turned the shower on until the
bathroom was consumed in steam. I disrobed, then stepped into
the hot water and felt every scratch and soon-to-be-bruise from
the fall. I let out a gut-wrenching cry. I cried for my father. I cried
for Oscar. I cried for my mother. I wish she would have been a real
mother so I could have had her for strength. The thoughts of not
ever having a mother made me cry even harder. Thinking of being
in the world truly alone was enough to rock my very being. I had
never given any thought to being without Daddy. I had just lived
my life never knowing being alone until now.

The water was stinging my body as it beat against my tender
skin. I stayed there for the better part of an hour before the water
ran cold and I emerged a different woman. I went in confused

and drowning in my own thoughts and sorrow. I got out on some different shit. That bitch in me was kicking some knowledge in my ear and I was ready to listen to her. She was on some revenge shit. I didn't give a fuck about what anyone thought of me from then on. I was gonna' seek revenge. I would have my day and I was gonna' have all that I wanted. Someone was playing a hell of a game and I had to be the winner if I wanted to walk away with my life.

I wrapped the soft, over-sized, towel around me and headed for the bed to lie down. That idea was quickly interrupted by a knock on the door. Grabbing my purse, and retrieving Chase, I inched to the door as quietly as I could. After seeing it was Epps I opened the door. Epps wasn't alone. Dread was standing to his right. He was still in his suit from earlier that day and he looked worn out. Epps finally spoke up after watching Dread and I eye each other.

"Ms. Clayton, he insisted that he needed to talk with you. I checked him. He is unarmed." Epps said.

I stepped to the side and let Dread enter the room. I informed Epps that I would be ordering room service and that no one else should bother me unless it was my brother. He shook his head and backed away from the door. Pushing the door closed, I turned to face Dread who was standing watching me.

"You know you could have told me who you were and what you had going on before I started giving a fuck about you YaYa." He scowled.

I couldn't believe he was going to actually stand there and try and give me the third degree after all that had gone on. I felt like I was living in a real live episode of "Snapped." Before I could unleash my pent-up fury on his smart mouthed ass, he moved to me and kissed me. His mouth was warm and inviting. It tasted the same way it did the first time we kissed. The hint of cinnamon was dancing around his tongue and I started to feel all of the tension leave my body. I knew I was wrong, but I didn't care. I didn't give a fuck because I had already decided to live each day as if it was my last. I kissed him back.

He reached under my towel and squeezed my ass. His hands were rough, and it felt good against my moist skin. I knew right then it was on. Fuck NiQue and what she thought she felt for him. The moment before me was about forgetting about all of the shit happening to me. I let go of the towel that I had wrapped around my body and pushed away from him so he could get a good view of what he was about to enjoy. No words were spoken, I dropped to my knees right there in the front room of the suite and released his massive dick from his suit pants. He threw his head back and groaned as I slow stroked his thickness in my small hand. He unbuttoned his shirt, and I reached up and ran my free hand down his chiseled chest and stomach. I felt him shiver with each stroke and touch I gave to him. I looked up into his eyes and parted my lips and devoured all ten inches of him in my mouth. I took him deep into my throat and rocked with him as he began to pound my throat as if it were my pussy. I kept up with each stroke and enjoyed watching him as he made fuck faces while he fucked my wet mouth.

"Damn girl," was all he could manage to say over and over as he pumped harder and faster with each stroke. I flicked my tongue all around the head and made sure he could see each time my tongue danced around his engorged head. I could taste all of his pre-cum and decided that I was going to get mine too. I rubbed his balls and caressed them while he fucked my mouth and grabbed the back of my head; guiding me to suck him off the way he liked. I flicked my clit just to show him I was gonna be his stress reliever too. He was gonna' remember this moment. He was going to get what I had wanted to give him since the first time I laid eyes on him.

Dread pushed me away from him, not wanting to cum without getting the pussy. He pulled me up off of my knees and led me into the bedroom portion of the suite. I walked past him and got up on the bed and lay on my back. I spread my thighs and fingered my drenched pussy. That shit must have drove his ass crazy because he got on the bed and scooped me up and turned me over. I got in the infamous doggy style position and anticipated his entrance. Dread slid his body behind mine and reached around my body and pinched my nipples. My body was almost orgasmic with just that one touch. He released my swollen nipples and wrapped his hand around my throat; entering my wet pussy. He was so big that I could feel him stretching my walls to their capacity. I knew what it was like to feel pleasure and pain in one thrust. He pushed himself into me as far as he could go, and I could feel the tears forming in the corners of my eyes.

"Oh shit." I yelped in reply to the serious dick he was giving me. He released my throat and grabbed my hair pulling me into him. He licked my neck and forced me to take all of him.

"Gimme this pussy!" He grunted while fucking me hard. Pushing back onto his dick, I let loose. I came all over his dick. I didn't want the wave of ecstasy I was on to end. He pushed my head down on the pillows and smacked my ass. I jiggled my cheeks to show him I wanted more. In return he smacked my ass harder. The stinging of the spanking was heightening my arousal. I came again.

I was not going to be out done. I crawled away from him and pushed him onto his back and licked all of my juices from his thick wet member. He moaned and pushed himself upward towards my lips. I knew he was well on his way to entering bliss. I licked his dick clean and mounted him. I rode his dick backwards so he could watch as my tight pussy swallowed his huge dick. I bounced up and down as he smacked my ass causing me to cum all over again.

"Oh shit baby, it feels so good." I moaned.

Now, he was slamming me down on his dick.

"Fuck YaYa, I'm cumming!" He moaned.

I felt his body stiffen as he exploded inside me. I continued to bounce up and down until he was practically begging me to stop. I came hard again and rolled off of him. I pulled the covers over myself.

Breathing hard, Dread stared at me. "So, now what?" I asked only half caring about the response.

"Girl, you are off the hook." He chuckled, trying to catch his breath.

"I guess we could start over by you telling me what the fuck is going on."

He reached for his pants and pulled out a tube that looked like a prescription bottle. The tube contained the prettiest buds of O.G. Master Kush I had ever seen. He twisted up a J and I proceeded to tell him from beginning to end what had happened. Well, I did leave out some stuff. There were some things he just didn't need to know.

I told him about Daddy and what line of work we were in. I told him how Neko entered the picture, and I also told him about Papi and how he may have had something to do with Daddy's death. I explained that Papi had forced me to leave the club with him the night we had met. After telling him all that I could, I waited for him to say something. He just looked at me like I was making up shit.

"You don't believe me do you?" I asked him.

"It's not that I don't believe you, it's just a lot to take in. You got a lot of shit going on baby girl. The question is how do you get out of it?" He finished.

"I hadn't put much thought to it. I don't even know where to begin." I said biting my lip. I didn't know what I was going to do. The one thing I did know was that there was going to be more blood shed.

"Well, you better do something because you got niggas hunting for your ass and you better get them before they get you!"

I took a pull from the blunt and pondered on his last statement. I needed to put some thought into who was gunning for me. For all I knew, it could have been someone close to me. It could have been any number of people. I exhaled and let out a plume of smoke. I felt my stomach growl and decided that I better eat something because I hadn't had anything all day. We ordered room service and Dread decided to stay with me through the night because being alone was not an option. I felt safe with him there. We made love all night long and I finally drifted off into a peaceful slumber. I had slept for what felt like hours, when my cell started to dance across the night stand next to the bed. Still half sleep, I grabbed my phone and saw that it was Neko calling me.

"Hello." I answered groggily.

"YaYa, some shit just went down around NiQue's people's house and I had to get out of there fast." He said between breaths.

All I could think was, *not again*. I looked over my shoulder to make sure I hadn't disturbed Dread. After ensuring he was still asleep, I got out of the bed and left out the bedroom and into the living area of the suite.

"Where are you now?" I asked Neko whispering into the receiver.

"I am in a cab headed to your hotel." He responded.

"What happened?" I asked frantically. I really didn't want to hear any more bad news, but I braced myself for the inevitable.

"I can't explain that right now." Neko said. "I'll be there in under ten minutes." Then the line went dead.

I went straight to the hallway to find Epps and let him know that Neko was on his way to the hotel. I also had Epps go down to the front desk and make arrangements for Neko's stay at the hotel. I had made up my mind that we could not be separated. Once Epps left, I started to make my way back to the bedroom portion of the suite. I was surprised to see Dread sitting up in the bed smoking a J with a puzzled look on his face.

"You like disappearing without saying shit?" He asked.

"Naw, my brother called my cell and I had to speak with Epps. Something happened and my brother is on his way here. He didn't wanna talk over the phone.

A defeated looked spread across Dread's face. I could see that all of my drama was not a good look for the rising star. He couldn't be associated with a slain drug lord's murderous daughter. He had too much to lose fucking with me. He got out of the bed and found his clothing that had long since been tossed to the side during our night of passion.

"YaYa, when you clean up whatever mess you're in holla at me." He said firmly.

"Rappers tell stories of their lives through their music. The thing of it is, I want to live long enough to tell the story. Fucking with you is dangerous. I got my career, not to mention my life, to think about."

He pulled his shirt over his head while I just stood there like a deer caught in headlights. I couldn't believe the nigga was carrying me because of some shit I had no control over. I stood in silence, dumbfounded, because I had no idea what to say. Part of me wanted to beg him to stay because I didn't want to face whatever news Neko had for me alone. The bitch in me wanted to shoot his ass for fucking me and trying to leave. I couldn't blame him though. I blew into his life and I am sure he could write a whole fucking album with just the shit going on in my life in one week alone.

"Aye, call me when you get this shit straight. You know how to get up with me." Dread said. He kissed my lips and exited out of the bedroom. I heard him leave out of the suite's main entrance as Neko was coming in.

I gathered my composure because I had to take in whatever news Neko had for me. I walked into the front living area and hugged my brother who had a look of shock on his face.

"What's going on?" I asked, stepping out of his embrace.

He made his way to the wet bar and opened the bottle of *Remy*. He didn't speak, he just took a swig from the bottle. I had no idea my brother was drinking too. The more I looked at him, the more I noticed that his being a part of my life was tearing him down slowly. He had bruises on his shoulders from where he had hit the dirt at Daddy's funeral, and his eyes were cold and had huge bags under them like he hadn't slept since the drama had all began. The innocence was gone.

"YaYa, after we dropped you here, I went to NiQue's and there was a shooting. They got her brother. They ran up in the house and got him. They stole all of the money and coke in the joint and shot him."

"Oh my god! Was anyone else hurt?" I asked.

"Naw. It was like they were going after him and him only. They knew where to find everything they were looking for. They didn't take anything else or fuck with anyone else. I don't even know how they got past the front door without us knowing. It was a set-up." He said taking another gulp of *Remy* from the bottle. He flopped on the couch and stared at me like he was waiting for me to have the answers.

"So, where was NiQue?" Is she ok?" I said, reaching for my cell phone from where I had left it from Neko's earlier call.

"She wasn't there. She left back out after we came in from Pop's funeral. She said she couldn't take anymore and needed to go out to think.

"So, where were you when all of this was happening?" I quizzed.

I had left out the house to get some green and when I came back to the joint, cops were all over the fucking place. With all the shit going on with Pop there was no way I could have the Feds ask me shit."

I sat down next to Neko feeling guilty. I had been sitting in my hotel room, while my brother and best friend were exposed to some shit that no doubt had something to do with me again. I was sexing my best friend's catch of the month, and she lost her brother. That nigga had taken care of NiQue since she was five; when their mother just left them for bad.

"So, I guess you haven't seen or talked to her then huh?"

My temples were starting to throb. I reached for the grinder on the table.

Neko shook his head from side to side. "Naw, I ain't talk to her. I called her phone, but she ain't answer. I started to leave her a message but that would have been fucked up to leave a message like that on her voicemail. I sent her a text letting her know she needed to get home and hit me up once she got there." There was silence and then Neko let loose.

"You gonna be real with me and tell me what the fuck is really going on? It ain't been nothing but death and destruction following us! I mean have you ever stopped to think about any of this shit or are you up here in this room moonlighting? Who knew where to go? Who would have access to Pops and Oscar like that? Who the fuck knew NiQue's peoples like that?" I didn't know how I hadn't seen it before. It had to be someone on the inside.

No one knew where the funeral was to be held. No one knew where NiQue's brother stayed but people on the inside. Someone close to me was doing some unforgivable shit. NiQue loved her brother more than anyone could imagine. They were all each other had. She was going to be devastated when she got the news. I split the blunt I had intended to roll and emptied the guts into the waste basket. I finally spoke on it. "It has to be someone who knows us all." I said, replacing the tobacco with some Chocolate Tie I had sent from California. Just as a pre-caution, I lit an incense and put the J in the air for Daddy and NiQue's brother.

The more I inhaled, the clearer shit seemed. I passed the Dutch to Neko. If you would have told me a week ago I would been smoking some Kush with my brother, I would have laughed at you. I guess there was some shit going on in his own world that he was running from too. He was inhaling the potent weed with no problems, so I knew it wasn't his first time smoking Kush.

There was silence again. I hated when it got silent like that. It felt like a void that needed to be filled. I started to drift into my high. One by one the people closest to me were having their lives torn apart. At first I thought it was because of Papi. I took care all of the loose ends with him so I know it wasn't him, unless some bitch was out for revenge and knew we were fucking around. Damn though, NiQue and her brother had nothing to do with that.

Someone was dismantling everything my father built and I had the misfortune of finding out who and why before they came for me and my brother. I knew that shit was bound to happen soon. They already tried once. What was going to stop them from trying again? I was too wired to fall right to sleep and Neko didn't seem like himself at all. We smoked and drank the rest of the bottle of *Remy* until the sun came up.

CHAPTER 22

The Stadium Nightclub
Queens Chapel Road
NE Washington, DC

I had finally drifted off to sleep when I awoke to Neko shaking me. Once I was able to focus on him and what he was trying to say. I sat upright on the love seat where I had fallen asleep. Neko was handing me his cell phone and I could read on his face that it wasn't a good call. I looked at the screen on the phone and recognized NiQue's number. Before I could get the phone to my ear I could hear her sobbing on the other end of the receiver.

"Hello." I whispered groggily into the phone.

"YaYa they got him." She cried, barely audible.

"Where are you? I am getting up and getting dressed right now."

She told me she had just left the police department and wanted to know where she could meet me to talk. I didn't know who was following her or would hurt either me or my brother. I couldn't have her come to the hotel and lead niggas right to me. I told her to meet me at the Jaspers in Largo. Between her sobs and sniffles, she agreed to meet me in an hour as she hung up.

Neko took the phone from my hands and retrieved the duffle bag he came in with the night before. He sat the bag on the coffee table which was positioned between the couch and love seat where we had been resting. He began pulling items out of the bag and pulled out a nine millimeter glock and sat it on the table. He gave me a menacing look when he saw me glaring at him.

"I'll be ready in a few minutes. You know you need to get ready to leave, so don't slow poke around."

I couldn't believe he was still talking to me like he was pissed at me. I started to tell him he better watch who he was barking on, but before I could even get my mouth open to tell him he better check himself, he looked at me square in the eyes. The look he gave me, made me shiver. If looks could kill, my brother would have murdered me. He walked off into the bedroom and I heard the bathroom door close and the shower come alive. I guess that was his way of saying he was riding out with me to meet NiQue. Once Neko was done showering and changing, I had already picked out a pair of *Seven* jeans and a casual blouse. I didn't want to wear anything too flashy or that would draw any un-necessary attention to me. I bathed quickly, got dressed, and headed to the front area of the room. Neko had already let Epps know we needed to leave. I felt like my brother had stepped into Daddy's shoes and had taken charge. I was relieved that he had taken the reigns, but he seemed cold and sinister towards me and I wasn't feeling it. Before he could walk into the hallway, I grabbed his arm.

"I'm sorry Neko. I was supposed to protect you and take care of you; not put you in harm's way."

"I know YaYa." He said dryly and walked out past me into the hall and towards the elevators.

I could feel my blood beginning to boil because he wasn't going to keep treating me like this shit was all my fault. I know he was feeling a certain kind of way about Daddy, but he had to know I wasn't feeling real good about any of this either. I couldn't handle him treating me so cold. We exited the hotel and drove in silence. It wasn't a long ride because it was a rainy Saturday afternoon which kept most of the travelers indoors. We arrived at Jaspers and met NiQue at the curb as she was heading inside. She had on a pair of *Jackie O* shades even though it was rainy and cloudy out. That meant she had been crying, high, or both. We were seated and ordered drinks and appetizers. I wasn't very hungry, but I ordered something anyway. I couldn't just sit and wait for NiQue to say something. I had to know what happened.

"So, what do the Feds think happened?" I asked trying to break the ice.

The waitress walked back to our tables carrying our Mimosas and sat them in front of us. NiQue waited until she had walked off before she started to speak.

"They think it's just another body dropping in the hood. They don't care. Trinidad Avenue got niggas dying daily. They don't give a fuck about one more." Her voice was weak.

She stirred her drink with her straw nervously.

"He was all I had." She continued.

"We understand." I said thinking about my father.

"At least you have each other." NiQue shot at me with hostility in her voice.

The waitress came back with the appetizers, momentarily breaking up the tension.

I knew that NiQue was taking shots at me, but under the circumstances I was willing to take it. She did just lose her brother. I understood her pain. She had the right to lash out. She just needed time to wrap her mind around what had happened. I just didn't want her thinking it was my fault. Even though deep down inside, I had the sinking feeling it was my fault. I knew the whole mess had something to do with what was going on with me and my family. The waitress placed the appetizers on the table and took our orders for the main course. Once we had ordered and the waitress had finished making eyes with Neko, I focused my attention on NiQue again. She was pushing the celery around the plate that came with her buffalo wings.

"What did any of this shit have to do with me and my brother YaYa?"

I had just about enough of being questioned by everyone; the police, Neko, Dread and now NiQue. What made it so bad is that I had no fucking answers and they were all expecting me to have some type of explanation or game plan. I had nothing but frustration building. My anger, and my sorrow for all the lives I had impacted with this shit, was almost unreal. I wanted someone to make it all stop. Just hit rewind on the hands of time and take me back to before all the madness started.

I snapped out of my thoughts and looked NiQue and Neko in their eyes. With the disappointed look they both gave me, I made up my mind that I wasn't going to just let people think I was losing my grip. I had to remain calm and try to focus on getting out of this shit alive.

"I am trying to figure out who did it and I may have an idea." I lied.

I stared at the last two people on earth who loved me and told a big fucking lie. There was no turning back know, they were counting on me to finish this shit. How the fuck could I finish it if I couldn't even figure out who amongst us hated me that much to cause the chaos.

"You will have to stay with me in the hotel so we can be together. I will arrange to get you both rooms."

NiQue's eyes became cold and calculating. "So, what are we going to do, just post up in a hotel while you pretend you know what is going on?" She snapped.

I was stunned with her hostility. I had done nothing but try and protect them. I just wanted to keep them close to me so no harm would come to either of them.

"No!" I stuttered.

"I just thought it would be better if we stuck together because obviously whoever is after us knows we are vulnerable apart. Plus, we would have Epps and his men there to protect us."

"Face it YaYa, you have been too busy in that nigga Dread's face to even try and figure out who is killing everyone we love!" NiQue was pissed. She didn't care who was looking at her.

It was all coming out now. She wasn't upset about what was going on with people trying to kill us, she was pissed about me and Dread.

"Look NiQue, I know you are hurting just like the rest of us, but Dread has nothing to do with this! I think you should keep your voice down before people get suspicious." I said looking around nervously. It was too late; people were already looking in our direction.

"Oh, shut the fuck up! "She yelled at me. Pushing away from the table and standing up, peering down at me. Her eyes were like daggers.

"You know what your problem is YaSheema? You are a spoiled little bitch that tries to use that over-worked pussy to get whatever you want. Well do me...no, do "us" a favor and use that rotten twat of yours to find out who killed my brother! You know you actually are a manipulative bitch. I thought when you let me fuck you it was because you actually loved me. You only did that shit to please yourself. You never thought twice about how I felt about you."

NiQue's outburst had the entire restaurant watching our every move. I couldn't sit there taking her verbal attack any longer. Before I knew what had come over me I had jumped up and lunged at NiQue. I smacked her so hard my hand stung from the impact. Neko jumped up and got in between us before NiQue could retaliate.

"Have both of you lost your fucking minds in here?"

He grabbed me firmly by my arm and pulled me to the door of the restaurant. I was screaming and hollering for him to let me go the entire way. There was no way she was going to put my business in the streets like that and get away with it. I was through playing with her. I knew she was going through her own hurt and pain, but she had crossed the line with her bullshit. The last thing I heard my best friend say as Neko pulled me out of the doors was the most hurtful shit anyone could ever say to me and it let me know my friendship with her was over.

"I hope the niggas who are gunning for your ass find you and bury you with your scum bag of a father, and that whore of a mother of yours bitch!" She spewed.

It took everything in me not to break free from Neko and whoop her ass in the middle of the dining area where she stood holding her bruised face. I looked at all the patrons who had just come to Jaspers to have their lunch, but who were looking at us in horror; and shot NiQue one last glance before storming out the doors. She had the nerve to have a smirk plastered across her face. She looked extremely satisfied with what she had done. As soon as we got in the car, Neko's cell phone began to ring. He answered it before the first ring was finished.

"What kind of shit was that you were trying to pull in front of all of those people he started to yell into the phone? Do you understand that we are in the middle of a war with God only knows who, and the police are just dying to bag one of our asses, and you go and pull some stupid shit like this."

I knew Neko was talking to NiQue. I, on the other hand, was behind the steering wheel wishing I could just back over that bitch with my car. She was supposed to be like my family and the shit she exposed was not even forgivable.

"Look NiQue, I want you to get some clothes and go check

into a hotel somewhere. Once you get there call me and let me know where you are. I will be there as soon as I get YaYa back to the hotel safely. You two are tripping, making a scene in front of all of those people, and both of you bitches got some explaining to do." He hung up the phone and just looked at me like I was crazy.

"Why are you still sitting here like that shit didn't just happen? Drive the fuck off before those people call the fucking cops." He said sternly.

I did as my brother said and backed out of the parking space and pulled off. I felt uneasy. I knew he wanted to ask me about what she had said about us fucking and about our mother. I could barely compose myself enough to drive, let alone answer any questions about my bitch of a mother and her disappearance, and me and NiQue sleeping together. I drove all the way to the hotel in silence. I didn't even notice that we had company the entire ride back to the hotel. I was sizzling on the inside. I pulled in front of the hotel and hopped out. Just as the valet was coming to park the car, Neko took the keys from my hands and got in the driver's seat.

"Where are you going? I asked. I really didn't need to ask because I already knew the answer to that question. He was going to question NiQue about all the shit she said today and I couldn't let him find out anymore.

I started to sob. "Don't leave me!" I cried out. "I can't be alone. Too much has happened to us and I cannot handle this shit on my own."

It felt good to tell the truth. I had finally let down my guard a little bit and told Neko just enough to try and make him stay and not get the rest of the story from NiQue. His eyes softened from seeing me cry. I had put up a front so long that he could see that I was scared, tired, and confused because I was crying. He gave the keys to the valet and escorted me to the doors of the hotel.

We walked through the lobby to the front desk and got another room just below mine. We registered him under another name because the police were looking for him to question him about the shit with my father, and other niggas might be looking for him to get to me. My mind was racing a million miles a minute. I was trying to think of how I could avoid explaining all of the shit NiQue had said at lunch. Neko was all I had left in the world, and I needed him to remain on my side. I didn't know how he would look at me if he really found out that what NiQue said was all true. We rode the elevators up to my floor and we walked pass Epps.

I gave him a nod and he nodded back, letting me know that everything was safe. I used my keycard to enter through the doors and I could tell that housekeeping had been in to clean the room. The room was neat and looked as though no one had stayed there. I dropped my belongings on the coffee table and flopped on the couch, kicking off my shoes. I ran my bare feet through the plush rug. Neko made his way to the bar and poured himself a drink. He made his way back across the room and sat in the recliner across from the sofa where I was seated. I knew it was now or never because the moment had come to give him some type of explanation for what NiQue had exposed. I wasn't going to volunteer any info if I wasn't asked.

Neko took a sip from his glass and sat it down on the table. He watched me while I tried not to look him in the eyes in fear that he would be able to tell that I was holding so much back from him. I could tell he was not going to force me to speak, but he was definitely going to sit there and wait for me to say something. He didn't care how long it took either. He had already made up his mind that I was going to stop bullshitting him. It was like playing a game of chess. It was a true test of wits. I wasn't trying to make a move and lose the game, and he was going to wait me out move for move. A few more silent tense moments passed before he finally spoke.

"So how long are we going to sit here trying to get around the shit she said?"

My eyes met his, and I started to tell him it all from the day I took my Mother's life in my bedroom for disrespecting us and trying to separate us. I wanted to tell him that I had watched Papi die and that I thought the reason we were targets was because of it. I wanted to get it all off of my chest. I wanted to tell him that I had made two huge mistakes, one by sleeping with NiQue and two by falling in love with Dread. I wanted to tell him that Corinne, Daddy, and NiQue's brother Sean, were all dead because of something I was twisted up in. None of that came out though.

"Neko, NiQue is grieving and she was just talking crazy."

The tears stained my cheeks as I tried to conceal the drama I had caused. I could tell Neko wanted to believe me. He was searching my face desperately for truthful answers and looked so disappointed that he was getting none. He shook his head and rose from his chair. He walked over to me and pulled me to my feet. He wrapped his arms around me.

"Whatever it is you need to tell me, I guess you will tell me when you think the time is right." His voice was full of sorrow like he couldn't trust me anymore, but he seemed too tired to even try and get the truth out of me.

"Look, when you are ready to talk, I will be downstairs. Just call my phone. I need to try and get some rest." I hugged him back not wanting him to leave me, but not wanting to talk about any of the mess I had created. He stepped out of my embrace and left the room. I felt relieved that he was not pressing the issue and going to try and get some rest. I needed to try and get some questions answered.

Chapter 23

The Bleu
Lanham, MD

I woke up to Epps knocking on my door which was weird because I hadn't even realized I had fallen asleep on the couch. I grabbed my cell and checked the time and saw I had slept for an entire day. Rubbing my eyes, I pulled open the door to the suite and Epps was standing before me looking a little concerned.

"What's going on Epps?" I questioned, not wanting to have a long drawn out conversation with him about any more bad news.

"Ma'am, your brother just left the hotel, he refused to let us accompany him, and he refused to let me inform you that he was leaving. As soon as I spotted him leaving, I thought I should let you know."

I began to pace back and forth. I knew where he was going and I didn't like it one bit. He was headed to NiQue. The only problem was that I didn't even know where she was. As if Epps knew my concerns, he spoke up. "I sent Debo to follow him just in case some shit popped off. I just wanted to let you know ma'am."

"Call Debo and find out where he is headed. Tell him not to let Neko out of his sight! If anything looks strange get my brother out of there."

"Yes ma'am." he said backing out of the room.

"Oh, and Epps…if we need to handle anybody and I do mean, "anybody" just be ready." I said before he could get out of the doorway totally.

I couldn't believe what had just left my lips. I would rather kill than have my secrets of betrayal out there. It was bad enough I had to find a way of fixing the mess with Neko. NiQue was sure to tell him all she knew about my mother's disappearance and God only knows what else. I was way past being concerned about NiQue. I was borderline ready to dead her ass. She knew way too much, and she was bitter. She was pissed because I wasn't into that lesbian shit and she was mad about Dread. The more I thought about it, she was more pissed about the fact that I didn't want to keep fucking her than she was about her brother, Big Sean, being killed.

I twisted up a J, turned on my *Ipod*, and sat it in the speaker holster on the end table. "Twirl Off" by Lucky Lamar and Dread filled the air as I blazed. The Kush I was smoking had calmed me. I had put just enough "fuck it" into my system to just deny anything NiQue said to Neko about my mother, about us fucking, and anything else she had to say. My cell phone buzzed and then rang out breaking my concentration on getting high. I looked at the name on the caller ID on the phone and my stomach started to churn. It was that damn detective. I reluctantly answered the phone. "Hello."

"YaSheema, this is Detective Gatsby. I wanted to know if we could talk. Three bodies of three people were found in an apartment building in Southeast DC."

My heart began to beat fast. It never occurred to me that no one had found Corinne and her company stuffed into the closet.

"Well, what does that have to do with me? I obviously don't live in Southeast DC." I said trying not to let on that I knew anything.

"Yeah Ms. Clayton, there was an eye-witness who put you at the scene of the crime." My face felt hot. Like someone had set fire to me. I began to sweat profusely.

"They have to be mistaken because I don't know anything about that."

Ms. Clayton, have you heard from your brother? We still need to talk to him about your father's murder and your uncle's attack. You know, as a matter of fact, a lot of folks associated with you and your family keep coming up dead. Would you like to talk about it? First your boyfriend, then your father and only God knows who else."

His voice trailed off. "As a matter of fact, either they come up dead or missing. I am starting to wonder if your brother and mother are even alive!" He had struck a nerve bringing up my brother. I could no longer contain my dislike for him and the way he was talking to me.

"Look detective, I don't know what is happening; I don't know where my brother, or mother are! I don't know who the fuck murdered my father and tried to kill my uncle. Any number of people could have murdered Corrine and her little bitches; she was a drug dealer, just like my late boyfriend!" I screamed into the phone. Before I could stop my chest from heaving up and down I realized I had fucked up royally. Gatsby realized it too, and began to laugh on the other end of the line.

"YaSheema, if you didn't know Corrine was dead, how did you know the other people she was found with were females? Better yet, how did you know that they were "friends" with Corrine like you said?"

I had to think fast because the pig was trying to pin me with shit I didn't even have anything to do with. "The streets talk detective. That is all I can say about knowing she was with her female friends. Besides, she was into women; I just figured it was her girlfriend. She didn't deal with too many dudes except for with business." I was hoping he was buying the bullshit I was feeding him.

"Mr. Gatsby, if you are done trying to ask me questions I clearly have no answers for, I will be going. I have yet another funeral to prepare for. Maybe you should focus your time, attention, and energy on the real killers instead of insinuating that I know more than I am telling you. Are you done?" I asked in a nasty tone.

"For now, but I am sure we will talk again real soon." He said with an air of confidence.

I disconnected the phone call before he could say anything else. My head was throbbing. I decided there was way too much going on for me, and I had to start making moves before anything else happened. I needed to be proactive instead of reactive. That shit was getting me nowhere. I left the sanctuary of the hotel room and got into my car. I knew where I was headed wasn't smart because anyone I loved was getting taken from me one by one, but I had to try and get some answers. I pulled up in front of PG Hospital. Oscar was doing better and it was time to try to ask him what he knew about who had tried to kill him. I walked inside the hospital and decided to go to the gift shop and pick up a few things for Oscar. I grabbed a few magazines, some snacks, and a couple balloons that wished a speedy recovery on the front of them.

After purchasing the items, I headed for the fourth floor and to the nurses' station. They pointed me in the direction of where Oscar was being treated. My heels clicked as I walked down the hallway. I hated hospitals. I had always wondered why they were painted in those awful colors. They were all the same; institutional blue, split pea green, and sickening yellow. The always smelled like death and decay. I entered Oscar's room and he was sleeping. I couldn't help but notice that he was hooked to several machines and there was an IV machine lightly humming. I took the items I had purchased and placed them on his bedside table. I tied the balloons to the bottom of the bed. When I looked up, I saw Oscar staring at me.

"Oh, Oscar I didn't mean to wake you. I pulled up one of the chairs and positioned myself where he could see me.

"Hey YaYa. You are a sight for sore eyes." He said weakly.

"So are you Unc? I am so glad you are alright. I mean, all things considered." I said. He tried to smile at me and I could tell he was in pain.

"Look, I can come back when you feel up to having visitors." I said not really wanting to go. He was one of the only people I had left that reminded me of my father.

He looked like he was worn out and like the lifestyle had broken him down. He sat up and started to speak. "Would you like to tell me what is going on?"

"Well Unc, I was hoping you could help me. Do you know who did this to you? Did you get to see who it was that day in the house?" I asked.

Oscar's eyes got wide as saucers. "No, I don't know who did this. It all happened so fast. One minute I was headed to move the car and the next minute I felt bullets ripping through my body like fire. I never saw their faces." His voice trailed off.

He looked so sad and defeated. I could tell that he felt like he had failed us. What he didn't know was that I was so glad that I didn't lose him too.

"YaSheema, I didn't see who did it, but they said something that I will never forget."

I sat to attention and concentrated on whatever it was that Oscar was going to reveal. The hair on the back of my neck stood up.

"YaYa they said they had come for you." He said sheepishly.

Before he could say anything else, the nurse walked in to take Oscar's vitals and administer his meds through the IV. I could tell he had more to say, but was leery of speaking in front of the nurse. I could see him fighting to stay conscious as she emptied the syringe, which I assumed was filled with pain meds, into his IV line.

"Ma'am, the medicine I just gave him is going to put him to sleep. I hate to cut your visit short, but he won't really be good company in about three minutes." She chuckled.

I am glad she thought that shit was comical because I damn sure didn't. I wanted the bitch to exit the same way she had come in. I desperately needed to know what else the killers had said. It was too late, the drugs had taken affect and Oscar was in a deep sleep and wasn't going to be telling anyone anything until he came to the next morning. The nurse left closing his door behind her. I rose and kissed Oscar on his forehead, careful not to touch his bandages.

"I promise that I am going to catch whoever did this to you." I whispered before walking out of the hospital room and out of the hospital altogether. I had my game face on and some niggas were gonna pay.

CHAPTER 24

The Fish Market
Old Branch Avenue
Clinton, MD

I didn't feel like going back to the hotel being that I knew Neko would be there waiting to ask me all sorts of questions about what NiQue had told him. I drove towards Dread's. I knew he didn't want to see me. He had made that very clear.

Through all that was going on he was the only little piece of sanity I had. I figured it was now or never. I had to tell him the truth. I found myself wanting to tell him everything that had happened. I wanted to be with him. I wanted to come clean with someone so desperately about all the crazy shit I was going through. I knew he would keep it one hundred with me no matter what. I pulled up to his apartment and almost didn't get out of the car. I climbed the steps, and once again I almost turned around.

Once I was in front of his door I could clearly hear voices. It was the last voice I expected to hear coming from Dread's apartment. It was NiQue.

What the fuck was she doing there?

I could hear her sniffling like she was crying and I wanted to know why she was there in the first place. I knocked on the door and covered the peep hole with my hand so he couldn't see me. He didn't even hesitate, he opened the door without even bothering to ask who it was. I pushed past him and was prepared for a showdown with my best friend. God only knows what she had told him, and it really ain't matter at that point because that bitch had pulled one too many stunts for my liking; she had to go. NiQue was faster than I thought and had jumped to her feet once she saw me. She had already taken a defensive stance and was ready to throw down in the middle of Dread's home.

"You sneaky bitch!" I yelled as I jumped on her, reigning blow after blow. She fought back wildly. Dread tried to separate us, but I guess we proved to be too much for him and we got around him. I shoved NiQue to the floor and sat on her, delivering punch after punch like we were never friends. The only thing that saved her no good ass was Dread pulling me off of her and dragging me out the front door.

"What the fuck is this shit you are trying to pull YaSheema?" He said through clenched teeth.

"I thought I told you to stay away from me. I ain't want no parts of whatever shit you are twisted up in."

He let me go and pushed me towards the steps leading to the front entrance of his building. Tears began to stream down my battered cheeks. I walked down the steps defeated. I turned to try and fix it with Dread. I tried to say what my heart had been leading me to say all along. I wanted to tell him the truth about what was going on, and I wanted to tell him I was falling in love with him. Before I could open my mouth, I saw NiQue standing behind him with a smile plastered across her bruised red face, and it made me re-think what I was about to say.

She was gonna be dealt with. It was war between her and me at that point. There was no use in fighting a battle with her right there when it was clear I wouldn't be the winner. She and I were going to face off eventually for her betrayal, my betrayal, and a lot of other things in between.

People started to open their doors to see what all the commotion in the hallway had been about. Before I had to face their questionable stares, I left. The only good thing that had come from my trip to visit Dread, was knowing that Neko hadn't been with NiQue finding out his sister really wasn't shit. I straightened out my clothes and got in the car. I looked in the rear view mirror at my reflection and couldn't believe that NiQue and I had let our friendship turn so ugly. We were fighting like niggas in the street. I was sick of the life I was leading. I was tired of running from an invisible ghost. Too much happened to go back. So it was time to eliminate all of the problems in a whole. I would just go, but not before closing up all my loose ends. I started my car, backed out of the space, and headed back to the place it had all begun. I headed home.

I sped up 395 trying to calm my nerves not knowing what would be waiting for me. I rolled through the streets of DC until I got into Georgetown and slowed only because the police in this district didn't take to kindly to uppity black folks. I moved in and out of traffic and through back streets until I reached my home. It looked cold and uninviting. It didn't look like the place where I had made so many memories; good and bad. I pulled up into the driveway and couldn't help but notice the yellow police tape by the garage. I tried to shake the nagging feeling that I should not be there out of my mind, and shut down my engine. I walked up the drive and for a moment I swear I could hear nothing but the gravel crunching beneath my feet. My hands were sweaty as I moved up the walkway.

I opened the front door and the pain flooded my heart. It was the second time that day that my heart had been abused. I looked through the empty foyer and saw my childhood. I saw me as a child rushing down the steps to greet my father when he would come home. I saw visions of us as a family, gathering our things to head out to have daddy-daughter time. The visions would not stop flowing through my mind like a raging river.

My mind was trying to process all of the memories that were flowing through it. I saw my mother invade my memories. It was the time before she really let the drugs take over her. She was beautiful, and her grey eyes sparkled. She truly looked like she was happy. She looked like she loved her life. In that instant, I saw her and my father embrace as if they were in love.

I shook my head trying to clear the memories from my mind. It was too late to try and get the past back. They were both gone. For the first time, I regretted killing my mother. I wished she could have been the mother I needed, the mother I wished she could be. I wanted her to love me more than she loved crack. I wanted her to put me first like a real mother should. Other children had their mothers to be there during their first day of school, when they started to like boys, to celebrate Mother's Day and birthdays. I wanted that. My father tried to give me whatever I wanted, but he could never give me a mother. He could never give me that normalcy I so longed for.

It was true that I had any and everything I could have wished for material wise, but I secretly longed for a real stable family with bonds that could not be broken. I didn't ask for drugs, money, murder and mayhem. I never asked for any of the shit I was dealt. My father bred me to want those things that had hurt so many. He taught me chaos. That was all he knew. He didn't know his teachings were going to be his downfall and the downfall of all the ones he loved so dearly.

The fresh hot tears streamed down my face. I was lost in a world I had not wanted. I didn't want my father to grow to hate my mother; and because he did, I did also. I wished that I could forgive her. Instead I had followed his lead and hated her for what she had become. Instead of helping her through her addiction, he threw her out of not only our home, but out of my life.

I braced myself against the banister leading up the stairway. I was feeling so lost in a place that should have been so familiar. Being in my father's tomb, my home was overwhelming. The more I tried to fight the demons surfacing, the more I was faced with them.

Flashes of the day I reunited with my mother were so bittersweet. I had dreamed of that day all my young life. Silly as it may have seemed looking back, I longed for my mother to come home to us clean and sober and ready to be a mother. Instead I got her back more strung out than ever, and ready to take away the only thing she gave me that appeared to be a gift; my brother Neko. She had brought him to us and then wanted to take him from me and I hated her for it. It was like she was on some get back shit. I had taken her place as the woman in my father's life, and she would take away the one thing I wanted more than ever, a semi-normal family.

I shook off the visions and walked up the stairs towards my room. I stopped in my tracks when I heard noises coming from Neko's room. I slipped my hand in my purse and pulled Chase out of it. I pressed my back against the wall of the hallway and moved silently. I didn't know what to expect, but I knew no one should have been in my house.

Once I reached Neko's room I mustered up all the courage I could find and pushed the door open. I froze in horror watching my father's most loyal employees rummaging through our shit. They were bagging up anything they could find valuable. I reacted to the betrayal and let off round after round into the two men's bodies. I didn't need to ask questions. There was no honor among thieves. They surely would have taken me out to steal from me. They knew Oscar was out of commission and they also knew that

I was supposed to be held up in a hotel under the careful watch of Epps. They must have never suspected that I would return home, and even if I had returned they would have been long gone with anything that wasn't nailed down.

Jew Jew, the bigger of the two men I had just shot was still moving on the floor. I stood over him. I am sure he could see the anger and hurt in my eyes. "Jew Jew, why would you steal from us? Who sent you here to take from my family? You ain't smart enough to come up with this shit on your own."

He laughed and coughed blood. "Bitch, where you are going you ain't gonna need none of this shit anyway. We don't work for you. We worked for your father not you." He groaned. I kicked him viciously in his side with my *Red Bottoms*.

"Why would you steal from me? What were you looking for in my brother's room? You might as well tell me because you are going to die either way! You might as well die with a clean conscious." I laughed as the insanity of everything had gripped me and wouldn't let me go.

"Bitch, I ain't no snitch, so you might as well kill me and figure that shit out on your own 'cause I ain't telling you shit." He muttered.

I kicked him violently in the spot where I saw the blood flowing from his wound. He groaned and tried to laugh as though it didn't faze him that he was going to meet his maker. The poor bastard had the nerve to recite Psalm 23:4.

"Yea, though I walk through the valley of the shadow of death, I will fear no evil: for thou art with me; thy rod and thy staff, they comfort me. Thou preparest a table before me in the presence of mine enemies: thou anointest my head with oil; my cup runneth over. Surely goodness and mercy shall follow me all the days of my life: and I will dwell in the house of the LORD forever."

I had had enough of him preparing to die and I surely wanted him to rot in hell. I didn't want him to repent for his sins in enough time to make it to heaven. He needed to burn and I was gonna make sure he was going to do just that. I laughed, being that the whole scene was hilarious to me. A big ass goon was now bleeding to death on my floor and praying for his salvation. At least he knew the end was near. Before I could even deliver another blow to his wounded abdomen he tried to speak. I couldn't make out what he was saying.

"Speak up you piece of shit!" I yelled. I was furious.

"Bitch, you are going to die and if she gets her way, you will join me in Hell real soon!"

I stepped up to Jew Jew's massive body and placed the stiletto of my *Red Bottoms* right in the wound that was gushing so much blood. I was sure he was going to die of blood loss at any moment.

"Arggghhh!" He screamed as I pushed the bullet further into his body causing him to gasp. I had to admire the fact that he didn't – not once during the whole ordeal—beg for his life. He simply prayed and talked shit waiting for me to finish him off. Now that is the heart of a real killer and the essence of a real goon! I almost admired the scum bag piece of shit. He had a lot of balls. I guess that is why my father employed him for the past ten years. I stopped thinking of what he had said. I looked down at him again. His eyes were rolling to the back of his head. I kicked him again.

"Oh no you piece of shit. You ain't gonna die just yet." He convulsed and his eyes opened wide like a deer caught in headlights. "What did you mean by, "If 'she' gets her way? Who the fuck is, she?"' I quizzed.

He laughed again; this time it was weak and I knew I was losing time. His life was almost finished and I feared he would never tell me what I needed and wanted to know. Obviously he knew who was trying to hurt me and my family; and apparently it was a 'she.' I aimed my gun right at his temple.

"I was going to leave it so you could have an open casket funeral, but now I ain't so sure they are going to even be able to identify your remains when I am finished fucking talk!" I screamed.

He started talking in circles. "Keep ya friends close and your enemies closer. Everything ain't always what they seem." He whispered and just like that, he was gone.

I was so furious that he didn't tell me who was after me, that I emptied the rest of the clip from my gun into his dome; splattering brain matter and bone fragments all over the place. I pulled the trigger until the gun just clicked letting me know the cartridge was empty. The clicking sound brought me back to reality; letting me know I needed to get what I had come for and get the fuck out of there.

I backed out the way I had come in, and I noticed the other goon, Timmie, was holding something in his hands that I hadn't been aware of when I had first come blasting into the room. I stooped down and pried it from his dead hands. I couldn't believe he was trying to steal Neko's birth certificate. What the fuck did he want that for? I looked over the document trying to see why it was so important to whoever was trying to off my entire family. There was nothing out of place, until I got to the line where it named the father on the birth certificate. It said Darnell Clayton. I knew that must be a mistake because I was Daddy's only child. Surely Christa would have told Daddy that he had another child. Especially that it was a boy. I knew I was Daddy's pride and joy; but he would have loved to have had a son. There was no way the birth certificate was real.

At that moment, I had way more questions than I had come with. Why hadn't Neko told me that he knew Daddy was his father? Why hadn't anybody told me that Neko and I shared both mother and father? Most of all who the fuck was walking around that knew all of that shit? I started to let wild thoughts consume my head. Maybe Christa wasn't dead and was making sure she got me back once and for all. I had to find out what the fuck was going on before I ended up in Saint Elizabeth's mental hospital. I was almost ready to check myself in at that point.

I stuffed the paper in my purse and walked out of Neko's room and headed to my own room. I gathered as much stuff as I could because I knew I would never be coming back. I made several trips to the car packing the trunk. I made a trip back to Neko's room stepping over the bodies that lay dead on the crimson carpet that was white at one time. I grabbed anything that looked important to him and shoved it into a luggage bag. Exiting his room again, I saw a picture of Christa on his nightstand. She was smiling, like she knew I was slowly going crazy and she was enjoying it.

I picked the picture up and threw it against the wall; watching it shatter to pieces. I marched back down the spiral stairs and headed to Daddy's office. I knew Daddy kept a large amount of money in his office, enough for me and Neko to get the fuck out of DC for good and never look back. Only problem was, I wasn't sure about the keys to the safe.

I figured Daddy thought our house would never be the source of an invasion so I figured the combo would be right there in his office. His desk was locked and I didn't know where the keys were to get inside. I picked the letter opener up off the desk and popped the lock to the desk drawer. After sifting through tons of paper and trinkets, I came across a set of keys that were pushed to the back of the mahogany desk. I clenched them in my fist and headed to the safe that was built into the wall of the shower in the bathroom that was housed in the corner of his office.

I slid the stained glass doors and removed the tiles on the wall revealing the safe. I dropped the tiles to the floor and tried each of the keys. After trying the first five I was starting to get antsy, like none of the keys would work. I tried key after key until I came to the last one on the ring and it slid in the chamber and turned effortlessly. I pulled the door open and my eyes were as wide as a six-year-old kid at Christmas. Inside the steel vault there were stacks and stacks of money. I ran from the shower and went straight to Daddy's closet and pulled out two bags and drug them into the bathroom and began filling them up with the stacks of cash. Once I was done stuffing the bags with the cash I saw a few documents that were at the bottom of the vault. Something told me to leave the papers right there, but whatever was in there Daddy didn't want anyone to have easy access to, so it must have been important to him. Grabbing up the papers I took them back into his office and sat down on the Italian leather sofa that was adjacent to his desk.

I began to read what looked like insurance policies. Not only had Daddy had hundreds of thousands of dollars in the walls of his shower he had his Last Will and Testament and insurance policies for me, Neko, and someone named Pajay Clayton. I had no idea who that was. Maybe it was a distant relative. I didn't know and didn't care. The policies were each for a million dollars in the event of his death. The strange thing was that the policies were effective and dated for years earlier which left me with a sour taste in my mouth.

Daddy knew Neko was his son all along and he never mentioned it to me! I felt betrayed. He had kept my brother away from me. He knew Christa had borne him a son, and he never even told me. My heart was breaking. My perfect father who had always kept it real with me had hidden so much. I was stunned. The day was officially turning into the worst day of my life.

I had to pull myself together because it was not the time to sit and wallow in my own self-pity. I still had two dead bodies in my brother's bedroom to deal with. I rose to finish the shit once and for all. Two pieces of paper had fallen to the floor. I bent to retrieve them from the floor and my heart damn near stopped. There was a hand-written letter from an unknown sender.

I began to read it and I am sure I lost all sense of reality.

Daddy,
All that you do in the dark will come to light. That precious daughter of yours is in for the fight of her life. You thought all of your secrets were safe and that you could keep running from them. Life as you know it is over! I plan on taking her pretty head, after I destroy your entire world, just like you did mine! How's that for Karma Daddy Dearest? I'll see you in hell!

Hate Always,
Pajay Clayton

Instantly I had a flashback. I knew that the letter had to be the one that Daddy had received the day we ran into each other a few weeks back. It was starting to make sense. Niggas weren't gunning for me for the shit I had done. They were after him! They were just using me as bait to get whatever it was that they wanted from Daddy. Whoever that *Pajay* bitch was, was the person Oscar had mentioned; and the "she" Jew Jew was talking about before I left him smeared on the floor upstairs.

I kept re-reading the letter in amazement; fear and panic started to take over. I jumped up, stuffed the letter and policies inside the bags and moved to the front of the house. I put the last of our things in the car and went back into the house by way of the garage. I found what I was looking for, the gasoline can. I was gonna burn that bitch to the ground. It was no longer a home. It was a lie. I ran from room to room making sure I poured gas on whatever I could until the can was empty. I made sure I bathed Timmie and Jew Jew real good because I didn't want any evidence of me doing them in. I lit a Djaram and took a few pulls and dropped it on Jew Jews stocky body before turning and walking down the steps and out the front door.

I had to move just like it was an ordinary day, even though the adrenaline was pumping through my veins. I had to force myself to walk to the car and pull out of the driveway as though nothing were going on. I got halfway down the block and heard what sounded like an atomic bomb go off. I didn't even bother to look back to see my life burned to the ground because at that point I simply didn't give a fuck! Oscar had some serious explaining to do. Game on!

CHAPTER 25

I nstead of going back to the hotel where Epps and whoever else may have been involved in the bullshit was, I headed across the Woodrow Wilson Bridge into Alexandria, Virginia. I had already decided that I had to lay low. I called Neko and told him to meet me in Old Town and to make sure no one knew where he was going. I had to stay out of DC because not only had I killed several people, but I had burned down my million-dollar home and had some unknown sibling out for blood too.

I knew I had to try and visit Oscar to find out all he knew about this *Pajay* person. He knew something. He was, after all my, father's best friend and confidant. As I sat in a *Starbucks* waiting on Neko, my phone interrupted my thoughts. I looked at the caller ID and saw it was Caesar. I hadn't talked to him since my father had passed. I didn't even know if it was still a good idea to do business with him with everything going on. For all I know he could be tied up in this mess and I definitely didn't want any beef with a Columbian drug lord. I still answered my phone, not caring what he had to say just because I would be gone in under a week's time and out of his reach, or so I hoped.

"Hello."

"Good afternoon YaYa how are chu'?" He said dragging his words in his thick Latin accent.

"I am well, all things considered. What can I do for you Caesar?" I asked not really caring what he wanted because whatever it was, I wasn't interested. Business was the furthest thing from my mind.

"I was wondering when chu' would be returning to work?"

"Caesar, it hasn't even been a full two weeks since I had to bury my father. Surely you can give me a little more time to get things in order with my family." I responded as I sipped on my latte trying to keep an eye on the door for Neko. It had been over twenty minutes since I had spoken with him and he should be coming in at any minute.

"I know chu' got a lot going on, but we have money to make out here. If you don't work, a lot of people on my side don't eat. I would hope it will take no longer than a few days. We have some catching up to do. Shall we say next Wednesday we meet?" He was doing more telling me than asking me.

"Sure next Wednesday is fine with me." I said knowing full well that that was one appointment I had no intentions on making.

"Good, so Wednesday it is then." Then the line went dead.

Fuck. Now that greasy dude had an attitude. I half ass wanted to laugh at the way he was talking about business as if we worked normal nine-to-five jobs. Just then I saw Neko walk in the door. He removed his shades revealing something I had never really seen before. He really did resemble my father. He looked like Christa more, but I could see my father intertwined. We made eye contact and he joined me at my table.

"So, wassup? Why couldn't we just meet at the hotel. Why did we have to meet all the way out here?"

I swallowed hard because I had to find out if he knew all along that Daddy was his biological father.

"I know we never talked about it much but, do you know who your father is and where he is?" I asked. Neko looked like he was caught off guard.

"Christa told me it was some dude that she met after she and Pop stop fucking with each other. She never really told me too much about him except that they didn't work out and after they split she found out she was pregnant with me. I never really cared to know because it wasn't like he was gonna' be bothered with me just because Christa was off the hook." He said sadly.

I felt horrible having to ask him all of that shit, but there were some things that just had to be done so we could find out what was going on. I took the birth certificate out of my purse and slid it across the table.

"I found this in the house today. There were some guys going through your room and I found one of them holding this in his hands. I was wondering did he find it in the house or was he bringing it to the house?"

"What do you mean there were some guys in the house?" He asked while unfolding the paper and growing quiet while reading the text. He slammed the paper back on the table. "What kind of sick shit is this? Who were these men who had this, and when did you go to the house? When did you leave the hotel?" He asked me question after question.

"Neko, did you know that Daddy was your father? Did Christa ever mention him before you met us that day at the park?"

He shook his head back and forth. Something deep inside told me he didn't know anything. He was just as clueless as I was. I knew Christa was in hell laughing for all of the chaos she had left us to sort out. Neko had a far-a-way look in his eyes. He slowly let his head lower and for the first time since I met him he looked defeated. He looked like he had been cheated.

"I know this is a lot of stuff to digest, but have you ever heard the name, 'Pajay' before?"

"No. Who is that?"

"I don't know who it is. I was hoping you knew who it was. After I found Timmie and Jew Jew ransacking your room, I broke into Daddy's safe and found three life insurance policies. One for me, one for you and one for someone named, 'Pajay.' Each one is worth over a million dollars a piece. Each one of them has been effective since 2003. Daddy knew about you, but he never spoke of you. I had never heard of this "Pajay" person until I found the policies and I also found this."

I handed the letter written by Pajay to Daddy to Neko. He scanned the letter and looked more confused than ever. "We need to go back to the house and try to find out what we can that our father hadn't told us!" He said beginning to stand.

I grabbed his hand and looked him in his eyes. "There is no house to go to." I said. "I burned that bitch to the ground after I shot Timmie and Jew Jew. I cleaned out the safe. I grabbed what I could and torched it. I had to. I left two dead bodies in your bedroom and niggas is already trying to pin murders on me that I ain't commit. I didn't want to have to try and explain to the police that I found two of my father's associates trying to rob us and that I killed them. They would have never understood. They are already gunning for me. They would not have wanted to hear that self-defense shit." I said truthfully.

"Look, all that back there is over; all we got now is us! We need to contact the insurance company and collect what's ours. Then we need to leave DC. The police are looking for you in regards to what happened to Daddy and Oscar. They are chasing me for some other shit that I am sure has something to do with whoever this "Pajay" person is. Whoever she is, she is on some *get back shit* and I ain't too fond of running from a ghost. You feel me? I don't know who she is. I don't know what she looks like. One thing I do know is that she knows who we are and she is trying to make me take the fall for all of this shit and I ain't about to let that shit happen!"

Neko finally looked hopeful. "So we are leaving here together? When are we going? Can we leave now? I am getting real tired of all this crazy shit going on. If I knew having a father in my life was going to cause all of this shit, I would have rather stayed fatherless." He said.

"We can't go just yet. I need to get at Oscar. I had gone to the hospital too. He knows something and before he could tell me what he knew, his nurse came in to give him his meds. Whatever she gave him put him back under and I wasn't able to get any info from him about who this bitch is. We have got to holla at him. He is all we have left to ask about who we are, and what is going on. He can at least tell us who is fucking up our lives.

"I think it is in our best interest to stay away from the hotel and Epps and the others; being that Jew Jew made it clear that most of them were working for whoever this "Pajay" person is and that she was not to be fucked with."

For the first time, I was really afraid. I didn't know who to trust and I was sick of running. I was running from enemies that I didn't know I had had. I was running from the police and from people who had been in my world my entire life. There was no way I could stay in DC. It was way too hot.

"Neko, there is something else too." His eyes were wide and wild. He looked as though he were at his breaking point. He couldn't take any more bad news.

"Daddy had a lot of money in that safe. I got it all before I closed up shop."

As I spoke those words, for the first time he looked hopeful.

"I grabbed what I could that belonged to you. I have everything I was able to carry in the car. I didn't even want to take the chance of getting a hotel room or going back to the city once I left Georgetown. I know that detective would have been all over my ass had I stayed. I think the best thing to do is to wait it out a few days, see Oscar and blow town. We have to be gone before next Wednesday. Caesar, Daddy's connect, is hounding me and I have no fucking intentions on dealing with that greaser."

Neko nodded his head in approval. "So how long do we have before we go and see Oscar? I figure the faster we see him and get the answers we need, the faster we can leave."

"I think the best time for us to try and get in to see him without too much notice is going right before visiting hours are over. If we go at that time there is less likely to be any police guarding him. Until later, we have to lay low. I suggest finding some place out here to get a hotel. Nothing fancy. Just a couple of rooms where we can rest. We also have to get rid of these cars because that stupid detective most likely already has an APB out on my Caddy.

I was feeling better with just knowing that in a few days we would be leaving DC for good. It hurt a little to know that all that my father had worked for was gone and that my life, as I knew it, was done. I said a silent prayer and hoped that God heard me for all it was worth. He and I have never had a good relationship, so I hoped he was forgiving like people said. I needed to walk away from everything with my life; and with my brother's life and freedom.

Our first mission was to get rooms. Neko and I decided that fancy, five-star hotels were out and we would have to settle for some *Red Roof* action to stay under the radar. I drove down route one in Alexandria and got two rooms under fake names. I paid cash so there would be no credit card linking us to the rooms; then I gave Neko the key to his room which was right next to mine.

We had unloaded everything into the rooms, emptying both cars being that we would no longer be able to drive either of them anymore. I had already called Benny to let him know I was coming to get a new whip and to have something nice for me to ride in. I wanted to take some time to try and gather my thoughts alone, but being that I was on borrowed time, rest would have to wait. Neko and I headed to Benny's garage. I was wondering what type of nice ride we would be getting. I would love to keep my Cadillac, but I knew it was too hot to keep it. It was one of the last things I had that my father had given me and I didn't want to give it up.

We pulled into the garage one behind the other. I was in my Cadillac and Neko was in Daddy's Benz. I had already pre-arranged for Benny to take both cars in exchange for one legit car. Neko and I had to stick together from there on out, or at least until we made it to our destination. Then we could get rid of the car that we got from Benny and each get our own separate rides. I stepped out of the car feeling lost. I knew I had just done the same thing a few months earlier, but it was definitely under different circumstances. Neko followed me to the garage doors and Benny greeted us.

"So, what will you give us for a Caddy and a Benz? Benny, I don't want a piece of shit either and it has to be legit. I need to be able to get on the road and drive it without any issues and no one taking notice of me."

Benny pointed to a black 2012 fully loaded Dodge Charger. "Will that do? " He asked.

Both Neko and I were satisfied with the exchange even though price wise we were getting dicked. Benny dropped the keys into my upturned palm and in exchange I had handed him the keys to my Cadillac and Neko handed him the keys to the Benz. I still felt a little cheated even though I really had no choice at the time. There was no honor among thieves.

I got into the car and started it up and listened to the Hemi roar. Neko got in the passenger seat and Benny handed me the spare key and the tag and title info through the window. Honestly, I could care less what we drove as long as we got the fuck out of there and fast. I waved goodbye to Benny and pulled away from his garage. Damn! Wherever we headed I would have to find another hook up man like Benny. He made shit so easy! Our next order of business was going to see Oscar.

Chapter 26

The Ultra Bar
911 F Street
NW Washington, DC

We pulled up to Prince Georges Hospital at about seven forty-five. Visiting hours were over at eight p.m. We had exactly fifteen minutes to get in there and find out what we needed from Oscar. Once we made it to the floor where Oscar was, we went to the nurses' station to make sure we were able to visit. I gave them my ID and signed the visitor's log. I gave them the name of the person we were visiting. The nurses looked from one to the other. They looked real uncomfortable.

"Ma'am I hate to tell you this but Oscar passed away a couple hours ago."

"No!" I screamed. "This shit can't be happening! What do you mean he passed away? I was just here earlier and he was fine."

"We still don't know what happened. We're really not supposed to release any information to anyone other than family." The heavy set nurse said.

"We are his family. He didn't have anyone else!" I yelled.

The elderly looking nurse stood and came from around the desk. She put her arm around me and led me away from the nurse's station.

"Ma'am, the doctors aren't sure, but they believed he had an allergic reaction to some of the medicines they gave him which caused him to have a seizure. They tried everything they could to bring him back. I am only telling you this because I have seen you here visiting with him. I am sure you cared for him. Now, all you can do is pray for strength to get through this."

I didn't want to hear anything about praying. I barely heard anything the nurse had said. I refused to let my tears fall. I was fucking sick of crying. I thanked the nurse dryly for the information and walked out of that hospital with Neko right by my side. We left there even more fucked up than we had come. We made it to the car and just sat there. I was tired of death hunting me, chasing me, and silently stalking me. Every time I thought I was moving ahead, another body dropped. It was like anyone I cared about was being ripped away from me.

Neko was behind the wheel of the Charger and was looking in the glove box for the parking ticket. A part of me was glad he was there because he may not have believed me if he had not been there to get the news with me. There was no way of finding out who the "Pajay" bitch was. Everyone who knew of her was dead. We left the hospital and dove the twenty minutes back to the motel. I decided to just leave all of the shit behind us. I no longer wanted to find out who was chasing me. I just wanted to put as many miles between us and whoever she was.

There was nothing left for us in DC. I never thought there would come a day when I would be forced out of my home because of fear. I didn't know anything about anywhere else. All I ever knew was DC. Sure I had travelled to other places, and I loved Jamaica, but DC was home and I had to leave it all behind. I had to take what I had left and never come back. There was nothing left to come back to. I simply gave up.

Neko and I pulled into the motel's little parking lot. It saddened me to know my last night in the DMV was going to be like it was. It hurt my heart because I couldn't even stay long enough to bury Oscar. I just couldn't be sure that we would be safe enough to pay our last respects to him. We would have to leave in the morning. We would try and get some rest and leave early, right after the traffic had died down from rush hour.

"So, we are done here huh?" Neko spoke up. I nodded my head. That was the first thing he had said to me since learning of Oscar's death. He got out of the car and walked up the stairs leading to the second floor landing leading to our rooms.

I don't know what made me do what I did next. I threw the car in reverse before Neko could even disappear into his room good. I pulled out of the parking lot and headed back across the bridge. I felt like I had some loose ends to tie up. I had to get some shit off of my chest. I found myself sitting in front of Dread's building even when I knew I should not be there. I mustered up all the courage I could find and entered his building for the second time in two days. I hoped he wouldn't reject me. I walked the stairs and knocked on the door. I heard him shuffling around inside.

"Who is it?" He asked from the other side of the door. I guess he had learned his lesson from just opening the door and not knowing who was on the other side.

"YaSheema." I answered.

He opened the door and stepped aside so I could come inside. I looked around nervously, my eyes silently asking him were we alone. He closed the door behind us and took a seat. I stood in place not wanting to get too comfortable because every time I did in his presence something always happened.

"I didn't come to stay long. I just wanted to tell you I was leaving." The words were barely audible as they left my lips.

Our eyes met and we didn't have to say a word. He knew all I wanted to say and I didn't have to say one single word. He may not have loved me, but he would never forget me. That was for damn sure. I had come into his life and wild shit had happened. There was no other way to describe it. Not just that ordinary – boy meets girl, boy and girl fall in love shit – either . He was mystified by me and that made him want to know more. He feared that knowing too much would get him killed. He stood and I tensed up believing that he was going to throw me out of his apartment again. I started moving towards the door.

"You don't have to put me I out. I just wanted to tell you I was leaving and I'm sorry. You and NiQue should try to work pass this shit."

He stepped in my path before I got to the door. "I can't fuck with her YaYa. I was telling her that that day you came here and ya'll got to rumbling in my living room. She was trying to tell me some wild shit about you that I could not believe. She said you could not be trusted." He paused waiting for me to defend myself.

I wanted to, but what was the use if he didn't want to deal with me. I was on the run and there was nothing I could do for him. The most I could do for him was get him killed.

"I don't know what it is about you."

He pulled me close to him and it felt like time stopped. I didn't know if that was a good idea knowing we were saying our final goodbyes. He kissed me. The tension that I was feeling left. I tried to back away from him.

"Dread, I don't know if we should do this again. I am already having a hard time saying goodbye."

He wrapped his arms around me and stroked my back. We engaged in a kiss that was so passionate my body was trying to react and tell him no, but my heart was telling me something totally different. I couldn't fight it anymore. I was in love with him and he was definitely feeling me. He led me to his bedroom. He undressed me and sat back on the bed.

DIRTY DNA

I don't know why I felt venerable being naked in front of him. I had been naked in front of him before but there was something different about that particular time. It was like he could see inside me. I had never felt anything like that before. I was sure that I would never feel that feeling ever again. I was open and he could have me. He stared at me before beckoning me to come to him. I walked to him nervously like it was my first time as he pulled me down on the bed with him. He took off his shirt and threw it on the floor with my clothes. Dread kissed all over my body. Sucking and nibbling on my nipples which were hard as diamonds. He continued to tease my body over and over. He was touching every inch of me, but the one place I wanted him the most. It was like he was starting mini fires all over my skin.

When he got to my thighs, I thought I would cum. Licking, sucking and biting my inner thigh until I just knew he could feel my heart pounding with insatiable desire. He left a trail down the other thigh. I bucked at his touch. I wanted to feel him. That teasing shit was driving me crazy. I couldn't take it anymore. I moved from under him and got to work; changing positions. I straddled across him just so my wet pussy was positioned right over his dick. I knew that first stroke was going to send electric waves through me. He could feel my slickness dripping on his manhood and he hadn't even stroked the kitty. Not being able to play a teasing game with him, I eased my chocolate kiss on him and gasped as he pulled me forward.

Catching a beautiful rhythm like we had been lovers forever, I placed my hands on his chest and rode out the wave of ecstasy. It was melodic. I couldn't do anything but hang on. My body felt like it was one with his. He caressed my body as he brought me to another mind shattering orgasm. It was like riding a rollercoaster where you're taken to what you thought the highest of heights and the orgasm was the thrill of dropping off into the unknown. It was that same feeling, where you are afraid but you keep riding, you love the feeling of letting go. That's what I felt.

He moved me from on top of him and got on top of me. He re-entered me and I could feel the tears gathering in the corner of my eyes. I didn't want him to see me crying over him. It wasn't my way. I couldn't keep the tears in place. They fell from my eyes and Dread kissed each one that fell, pushing deeper into me than I thought he could go.

"Damn girl, what are you trying to do to me?" he groaned. His body tightened and I was matching his thrusts. I wanted to make him feel as good as he was making me feel. I gripped the sheets as he lowered his head near mine and kissed my collarbone.

I whispered my response to him. "I am trying to make you love me the way I love you!" That was it. He was unable to fight the urge to cum and he came.

If I had died right then it would have been worth it. I was in love with him and now he knew. He was the one reason I didn't want to leave DC. I thought about asking him to come with Neko and me. I knew, deep down, that if I had asked him he may consider it. Before drifting off to sleep, I heard him whisper, "I think I am falling in love with you too."

We laid there until I drifted off into a deep, peaceful sleep. I woke up hours later with a smile on my face and Dread standing in the window watching the happenings on the streets below.

"Is everything alright?" I asked sitting up. I pulled at the covers that were twisted at the foot of the bed.

I must have startled him because he looked shocked to see me staring at him. "Everything is good. I hope I didn't wake you. I just couldn't sleep. I got some shit on my mind."

I stopped fidgeting with the sheets and walked over to him. I wrapped my arms around him and rested my face on his back pressing my bare body against him. "You care to share?" I asked.

"I never met anyone like you YaYa. I am so glad that you came into my life. I am just going to hate that you are going to have to walk out of it. I wish I could change the circumstances that are surrounding us."

"Well, can you come with us?"

"How am I supposed to do that? My life is here. My career is here. Not to mention my career is finally starting to head in the direction I want it to go." He turned to face me.

"You can continue your career from anywhere. You don't have to be in DC to have your career. I just can't be here. There is nothing here for me but you. My family is gone and all I have left is Neko."

I could tell he was in deep thought. I knew he wanted to jump ship with me, but he had so much to lose if he fled the area with me. "I can't say 'yes' to it right now YaYa. This is kind of sudden don't you think? I need some time to try and move things around. Do you even know where you are headed yet?"

I hadn't put any real thought to it. I didn't know where I was going to go. I knew it could not be some old country hick ass town. I still needed to live. I finally spoke up. "I don't know where I am going. I hadn't even thought that far ahead. I just know I have to go. I have to get out of town before I get caught up in some mess that I had nothing to do with."

"Well, why don't you lay low and figure out where you are headed first. Stay out of sight and formulate a plan. At least know where you are going to be headed. I cannot promise you that I am coming with you right this moment, but if I knew where you were going maybe I could visit or join you later."

I perked up with the thought of him joining me later. I needed to put some serious thought into where I wanted to go. I still had insurance money to collect and leaving at that moment might be detrimental in retrieving what my father owed me and Neko. Collectively, Neko and I were about to be two million dollars richer.

We needed that money to make a fresh start.

A few hours earlier, I had wondered if coming to see Dread was a smart idea, but being with him at that moment let me know it was a great idea. He knew how I felt about him and he made me step back and think some things through. I needed to get a better plan rolling besides just running from my problems. I had too much money at stake to just run. I had over four-hundred thousand in cash on hand, but the two million in insurance would make life somewhere else much sweeter. I could re-build and live good for a while. I started to relax just a little. I hopped back in his bed and hoped he would join me for another round before I went back to the raggedy-ass motel to tell Neko that we needed to hang around a little bit longer.

Dread and I sexed until the sun came up. He was fast asleep when I crept out of his apartment. I left a note on the pillow letting him know that I would be in touch and not to worry. I jumped in the car and headed across the bridge. I need to let my baby brother know we needed to figure out our destination and that we needed figure out how to collect the money due to us from our father, without our "so called" sister trying to murder us before we could collect.

CHAPTER 27

The Waterfront
SW Washington, DC

I arrived at the motel a little after 8:30 a.m. Neko was standing on the landing. He appeared to be mad as hell. A bit of remorse for my actions crept in the back of my mind. I knew I shouldn't have just rolled out without telling him where I was going. After all, I was the one who had made it clear that we needed to stay together at all costs. I knew it wouldn't be in my best interest to tell him where I had been. I didn't need, nor did I want, any more uneasiness between us. I got out of the car and walked up the stairs towards the room. Sliding the key in the slot and entering the room, Neko was right on my heels.

"So, it's aight for you to up and disappear and not say anything? If I do it, I bet you would be ready to lose your fucking mind!" He hollered.

"No, I was wrong. I shouldn't have left without telling you where I was going. I just drove around. I didn't go anywhere specific. I needed to get my thoughts together. I got to thinking we don't have a plan Neko. We don't even know where we are going to go once we leave here. We haven't even put any thought to the insurance money that Daddy left us either."

At the mention of the money, Neko calmed down. Once we were inside the musty room I took a seat on the bed and pulled the policies out of the bag. "We need to make sure we handle this first before we leave," I said dialing the phone number that was listed for the insurance company.

I lit a cigarette and waited through numerous options before I got to a live person. After verifying my information, the woman on the line verified the policy totaling one million dollars. She asked for a copy of the death certificate. I let her know I could fax that to her office. I jotted down some information and gave her my bank account information and she said that in about two weeks the money should arrive in my account. I inquired about Neko and she said she could only speak with him regarding the policy. I passed him the phone and I guessed that the lady on the line was taking Neko through the whole spiel she had taken me through.

Neko told the woman he had no bank account and that he would prefer that the money be sent to my account. The woman let him know a notarized letter needed to be faxed with the death certificate to ensure we were not trying to commit fraud. I made a mental note to make sure we got Neko a bank account as soon as possible. We both agreed that was a smart thing to do. Then it hit me to ask the woman holding our future in her hands if she could check the information for Pajay Clayton as well.

The kind lady on the line put me on hold for what felt like an eternity. I paced back and forth. I am sure I had worn a hole in the dingy carpet. Once she came back on the line she stated that she was not supposed to give me any information on that policy. I wanted to curse at her and call her ugly names for being so, "by the book." Before I could part my lips and throw insults at her, she did tell me that someone had called inquiring about if the death certificate had been sent in for the policies? She let me know that was all that she could tell me, and I thanked her for her time and hung up.

I was glad that I held on to my anger just enough to find out that *Pajay* was trying to get her hands on what she thought was rightfully hers. I rubbed my temples because they had started to throb with the thoughts of that bitch trying to take money after she had destroyed everything my father had worked so hard to get it. Then she had him taken out, just to get the money. What was even more puzzling was the fact that she knew that she had money coming to her.

Every time I started to think about all the things that Daddy had hidden from me, I started to feel sick. I questioned if he ever loved me as much as he said he did. The kind of betrayal I was experiencing was unforgivable. My stomach was churning. I had been feeling awful lately. I was sure it was the stress due to the severity of the situation. I focused my attention on Neko trying to hold the sick feeling at bay.

"I guess we won't be leaving here so soon after all." I said.

He nodded and left out of my room without saying another word. I was really getting sick of people and their attitudes when all I was trying to do was my best to survive. I sat down to try and ease the queasy feeling. I had way too many things swirling through my head. I felt like such a loser having to run with my tail between my legs. The only thing that seemed to be working for me was the fact that I was about to be richer than I could even imagine, and the possibility of Dread coming with me. Just thinking of him made me smile to myself. The churning in my stomach was starting to slowly subside and I turned over to try and get some much needed rest.

I woke up a few hours later and from the looks of things it was growing dark outside. I had slept yet another day away. I scooped up my phone and checked for any missed calls and messages. It was the same things. Epps had called trying to get my location so he could "protect" us. He had left several voicemail messages and texts. I guess at some point, he would have figured out that his services were no longer needed. I had also received a text from Dread thanking me for an incredible evening and that he could not wait to see me again soon. The last text I had came from a number I didn't recognize; and it read, "time's up!"

I threw the phone on the bed and pushed the eerie message to the left. I knew it was from her. I just didn't have enough energy to focus on who "she" was anymore. I figured the best thing for me to do was to lay low, collect our money, and get the fuck out of DC before the black sheep of the family killed us all. I laid there wondering what could have happened that had caused Daddy to never claim her. Apparently he knew who she was because he wouldn't just leave money to some person he didn't know. It didn't make sense. Maybe her mother was just a one night stand. I let my thoughts run wild wondering of who Pajay was and where she had come from and why she was after me. I had always wanted a sister or brother and now that I had both; I wasn't sure I wanted the sister. She damn sure didn't want to be bothered with me, unless it was at my funeral.

CHAPTER 28

Lux Lounge
New York Avenue
NW Washington, DC

Two weeks went by and Neko and I were really held up in the motel. We had sent off the information the insurance company required of us, and we were just waiting on the money to hit the bank. All we could do was sit and wait. I was feeling sick! I had been feeling really ill and I felt drained of all energy. It had gotten to the point where all I could do was sleep and feel nauseated. I was always tired and the never ending feeling in my stomach was starting to send me over the edge. Neko knocked softly on the door and I mustered all the strength I could to get out of the bed and answer it. I let him in and flopped back down on the bed.

"Damn, why you look like that?" He asked me with his face balled up.

"Look like what?" I shot back.

Needless to say, I had not been out of the room in about two weeks. I would get up to get small items I needed to survive, so I hadn't really looked at myself or bothered with a mirror for that matter. My days consisted of checking my bank account, waiting on that money to drop, and watching *Maury*. Neko's displeasure with my outwardly appearance showed all across his face.

"You need to get up and get out of this room YaYa. You look like shit. What are you doing just sitting in here eating? You look like you have gained about twenty damn pounds in here loafing around."

I smoothed my long t-shirt trying to hide my embarrassment about the way I looked. I ran my fingers through my hair which I had not taken a comb too. I just felt weak. I felt like someone had knocked all of the life out of me and I no longer cared about anything but getting out of the motel room with my life.

Neko was going on and on about us leaving and I could see his mouth moving, but I didn't hear a word he was saying. I was too busy fighting the urge to vomit. I had been doing a lot of that in the last two weeks. It hit me all at once that it was beyond time for Mother Nature to pay me a visit. I had been so wrapped up in laying low and getting the money that I hadn't even thought about my period. I figured going out to the *CVS* would do me some good anyway being that I had been held up in that room for weeks. I barely knew what day it was.

I gathered myself enough to head out to the store. I covered my eyes with my shades and walked out of my motel room door. Even with my shades on, the sunlight made me feel like I was being exposed to any and everything. I felt vulnerable. I moved quickly towards Neko's room and knocked softly. I had already decided to try and keep the peace with him by letting him know every move I made from there on out. However, I ended up making no moves. I stayed in the confinement of my room. Neko came to the door rubbing his eyes trying to adjust to the bright sunlight that was penetrating through the open door. He was shirtless with only his boxers on. He must have been sleeping.

"I was just letting you know I am going to make a quick run

to the *CVS* to grab a few personal things. Do you need anything while I am out?" I said.

He nodded his head and held up one finger as if to tell me wait. He closed the door and I could hear him shuffling around inside. I could also hear a female voice on the other side of the door. I was vexed about him having company when we were supposed to be on the low. I let the bad feeling I was getting go. Hell, if I wasn't embarrassed to be seen in the *Red Roof Inn* I would have had some company too. Maybe that is what I needed. Neko came back to the door. This time he was dressed in a t-shirt and some basketball shorts. I shot him a knowing look. He could read the displeased look on my face. I didn't even say anything I just shook my head.

"I was going crazy in here YaYa. You ain't been acting like yourself lately. You don't come out of the room and you ain't exactly been good company." Neko said trying to justify why he had a bitch held up in his room with him.

"Just make sure she doesn't run her mouth about where we are. As long as you keep your shit in order, then who am I to complain?" I said shrugging my shoulders.

"What do you need from the store?" I asked Neko with my hand out because I wasn't going to spend one red cent on him and whoever the bitch he had hiding out in his room was.

He passed me a twenty dollar bill. I stood there because he hadn't told me what it was that he needed or wanted from the store. I just stood there rolling my grey eyes at him.

"So are you gonna' tell me what you need or are you just giving me money to blow?" I asked sarcastically.

"I need some condoms and make sure you get *Magnums*." He beamed with pride.

I couldn't help but smile because my little brother thought he was the shit. At least he thought about protecting himself, unlike me. I didn't know what the fuck was going on with my body. I playfully punched him in the arm and walked away. Neko went back into his room to entertain his company as I walked down the stairs that lead to the parking lot. I still felt awful and I was praying that I was not pregnant. There was no way I was ready for a baby. Yeah, I was old enough, but with the way things were going in my life, a baby would not be a good idea. The father was torn between his career and dealing with me and my craziness.

I was feeling emotional just thinking of having a baby. What the hell would I do if I really had one? I drove the short distance to the *CVS* and started to feel nervous. I had never done anything like that before and for some odd reason I was scared. Deep down I knew I was knocked up, but I was hoping against hope that I wasn't. I didn't need the added stress of taking care of a baby on my own, because I am sure Dread would not be pleased with me being pregnant and leaving with his baby.

I walked in the *CVS* and felt so weird buying a pregnancy test and buying condoms at the same time. I knew that shit was like an oxymoron. I headed down the aisle that read, "family planning" and got Neko's Magnums first. I chuckled to myself because that nigga was a mess trying to play big willy buying Magnums. Right across from the condoms was the pregnancy tests. The advertisements boasted about being able to detect if you were pregnant days sooner than the other leading brand. There were some with multiple tests in the box. I didn't know which to pick. I picked up several brands and threw them in the basket to be on the safe side. I had heard about girls taking home pregnancy tests and them getting a negative and then nine months later a bitch had a baby. I was leaving nothing else to chance.

I left the "family planning aisle" and got the giggles all over again just thinking of the name of the aisle. There was nothing about planning in it. It was either you were trying to not to get knocked up, or you were trying to see if it was too late and you already were knocked up. I was hoping I was just scaring the shit out of myself. I walked the other aisles of the store to waste time. I didn't have much else to do but wait for my money. I gathered a few things trying to stall before going back to the motel and peeing on a stick to find out what my future held.

I walked around the store picking up shit I knew I didn't need. I threw ginger ale in the basket and crackers. I half hoped that they would make the nausea go away. I picked up tampons even though I had the sinking feeling I would not be needing them for the next nine months. I grabbed a few magazines and a pack of Djaram cigarettes. I took my items to the front of the store and two young girls were working. One of them had on too much makeup and the other had on too much perfume. The two of them together were a hot mess. The one with the overly made face was popping on a piece of bubble gum which I could smell a mile away. It was grape *Bubbalicious*. I thought it was remarkable that my senses were at an all-time high.

I placed my items on the counter and did my best not to hurl on the lady with too much perfume on. I could tell it was a cheap knock off, but who was I to look down on anyone. I looked like a worn-out mess and probably smelled just as bad too! I paid for my purchase and got out of the store right before I felt the bile rising in my throat. I made it to the sidewalk before letting go of the little bit of water and chips I had tried to hold on to from earlier. I heaved until my throat hurt. Whatever was going on with me had to end immediately because I could not stand feeling that way. There was no way I was going to be able to get on the road in a few days if I had to stop every few miles to throw up.

I collected myself and got in the car. I pulled out into traffic and I started feeling paranoid. I don't know why; I just did. I felt like someone was following me so I made sure to drive around and around watching my rearview mirror carefully to see if anyone was following my movements. After ten minutes of driving up and down route one in VA, I felt like I was by myself. I pulled into the motel's little parking lot and shut down my engine. The nervous feeling returned. I climbed the steps to the second landing and knocked on Neko's door. When he opened it, I was greeted with a thick cloud of smoke. I had already taken out the condoms so I didn't have reveal why I had really gone to the *CVS*. Neko took the Magnums from my hand and smiled wide.

"Thanks sis! I am going to need these!" He was way too excited about getting some ass.

I nodded and headed to my room. I was starting to feel anxious. I need to see what was going on with me. I slid the keycard and unlocked the room door and went inside. I noticed it was really dark. I guess because I kept the curtains closed so no one would bother me. I took off my shoes and headed to the bathroom with the bag of six tests. I read the instructions which were easy enough.

1. Pee on the stick.

2. Wait three minutes.

3. Decide if jumping from a ten story high rise is better than having a baby.

I guess I was so nervous I couldn't use the bathroom, so I drank three cups of ginger-ale and hoped that it would stay down long enough to make me have to go. After about thirty minutes of waiting, I finally had to go. I headed back to the bathroom and squatted over the toilet. I peed in a Styrofoam cup so that I could dip each of the tests in the cup. I was leaving no room for error. I placed two of the tests in the cup and waited. It seemed like the three minutes it took to get an accurate result was taking damn near forever.

I paced back and forth; I tried to focus on the television. I even attempted to smoke a cigarette. Nothing was working. Time was moving so incredibly slow. Finally, three minutes passed and when

I entered the bathroom I knew what was waiting for me before I could even get a good look into the cup. I pulled out the first test and it had a pink plus sign. I tossed it to the side because I had heard stories of women having false positives and I didn't want to be one of them crying and tripping for no reason. I pulled the second test from the cup and it had two lines indicating that I was definitely pregnant.

I knew one thing…I was not going to stand there like I was defeated. I threw the cup in the trash along with both of the used tests. I left out of the bathroom sat on the bed and tried to sort out what to do next. I couldn't help it. I cried. I was trying not to fall apart, but it was useless. I was breaking down, I was running from God only knows who and I was trying to protect my brother from some bullshit that Daddy had us twisted up in. My best friend hated my ass, so I couldn't even ask her for help or advice at that point. She wouldn't give me any advice being that I was pregnant by Dread. I was on the run and pregnant.

This shit should have been written in one of those stupid Urban Fiction books except it wasn't fiction. This shit was really happening. It was really my life.

I was confused on what to do next. The tears were flowing and I could not stop them. I am not sure if I wanted to stop them. I wanted someone to be there with me to hold my hand, rub my back and tell me it would be ok. I wanted to be able to tell Dread that I was pregnant and he would tell me which decision to make. *This is not how I imagined being pregnant.* I was confused and alone and scared. I cried until I had finally cried myself to sleep. I was hoping that the answers to all of my questions would come to me in my dreams.

CHAPTER 29

The Boulevard
Largo, MD

I woke up with a nasty taste in my mouth. I felt a little better after sleeping for a few hours, but I still had no idea what I was going to do. The only thing I knew was that I was not going to do, and that was abort my baby. I'm way too strong to even think that having a baby would defeat me. My real issue was whether or not I should tell Dread that I was pregnant.

I made my way over to the window and peeked out around the cheap curtains. It had started to get dark outside. I decided that I would see what Neko had to say about becoming an uncle so I left my room and went next door to Neko's room. I listened before knocking so I would not disturb anything he had going on. It sounded quiet so I decided to knock. I could hear him dragging himself across the floor. He must have checked the peep hole because he swung the door open wide and stepped to the side to let me in. I looked around the room half expecting to see the mystery chick I had bought condoms for to still be there. My guess was she was gone or Neko would have sent me packing. I took a seat on the foot of the newly made bed and Neko took a seat at the old desk that was across from the bed.

"So wassup?" He asked.

"I just wanted to tell you I got a lot going on right now Neko, and I need your help working all of this shit out. I went to the store today to buy a pregnancy test." I paused to see if he was listening to me.

He was actually staring at me like I was going to tell him that I was in fact pregnant and it was his child.

I continued. "I took two of them, and they are positive. I am pregnant. That is why I have been so sick lately." I blurted out.

I lowered my eyes feeling ashamed of what had happened. I should have known better than to fuck anyone without protection. I started to drift into my own thoughts when Neko moved over to where I was sitting and wrapped his arms around me.

"Awww…YaYa, that is great! I wonder what you are going to have. I wonder will the baby have our grey eyes. Will it look like Mom and Pop or will it look like the father?" His voice trailed off when I wasn't giving him any responses.

"YaYa, are you ok with this? I mean are you thinking about having an abortion?" He asked.

I shook my head left to right. "No, I think I want to keep the baby. I just may be raising it on my own. I don't think the father will be interested in having a baby with me. He barely even wanted to see me the last time we spoke." I said with my voice shaking and with me on the verge of tears again.

"Don't cry YaYa. I got you. All we need is each other. We can do this shit together. I don't even see what you are fretting for. As long as this bread hits your account soon, we can bounce and then we can get you some pre-natal care. We gotta' make sure we take care of my nephew!" He said excitedly.

Just hearing my brother being supportive made me feel a whole lot better about the situation. Neko hugged me tight.

"YaSheema, whatever we go through, we go through it together. I got your back." He said. I felt so safe in my baby brother's arms. I knew as long as we had each other we were going to make it through whatever storm came our way.

I was glad Neko was excited and ready for me to have a baby. I wasn't so sure it was what I wanted. What did I have to offer the baby besides pretty eyes and a keen fashion sense? I was born of a ruthless hustler, and the only things he taught me were: sex, drugs, power, murder and mayhem. I knew one thing: my son or daughter would not be brought up to believe that was how they were supposed to live their lives. If they did, they would end up just like me. I looked over at Neko and he was still smiling. He was really excited about the baby thing.

"We have to decide where we are going to relocate too. We never put any real thought into it. That money from the insurance should be coming any day now, and the day it comes, we should already have a plan about where we are gonna' go." Neko said.

"I was thinking we could go someplace sunny and warm." I finally said. I was feeling hopeful.

We tossed ideas back and forth about where we should go. I was set on Atlanta because it was far from DC and in the south, but it wasn't really country like going to South Carolina. Atlanta was busy, just like DC yet with southern charm. Neko, on the other hand was thinking Texas, Florida or Louisiana. I was against all three. I wasn't feeling Texas because I just kept thinking about cowboys and racist people who didn't like rich black folks. I wasn't going anywhere near Louisiana because of Hurricane Katrina. After she took aim on the Gulf Coast there was nothing in this world that could convince me that living in that state was safe. I was almost feeling Florida because of the heavy drug trade. I knew I could fit right in there and feel right at home, but the weather kept me from committing to Florida. They always had a storm or something brewing. So that shit was out too.

Neko and I sat up all night trying to figure out where we would go to live and raise the baby. We kicked around several ideas on what we wanted to do once we left here.

"I was thinking that if we settle in Atlanta I can set up a little boutique. I am sure I could learn those country, outdated hoes a thing or two." I laughed.

"I could open a car detailing shop and make cake in the south. You know how those southern bammas like to keep their whips fresh. I mean I could hook them up with the candy and custom paint jobs, rims and everything." Neko said daydreaming.

I sat back feeling good about the fact that we were mapping out our future and it had nothing to do with the drug scene. We were both eager to get the hell out of DC alive and not trying to establish a drug empire somewhere else. Although it was what I was taught to do, I just didn't want any parts of it anymore. I had someone else to live for now. My mind drifted back to Dread. Atlanta was the place to be for aspiring artists, so I knew he may consider coming along. He had even said that his boy, Lucky Lamar, was based out of the A.

I was starting to feel at peace with all of the decisions I was making and I just wanted to hurry up and execute my plans. I rubbed my belly and said a silent prayer for my future and everyone in it.

CHAPTER 30

Crystal Skates
Temple Hills, MD

Time felt like it was moving slower than molasses. I was growing restless. Neko and I had settled on moving to Atlanta. I was more than ready to go. Days had passed and still no money in my account from the insurance company. I had called them to confirm they had received all they needed to make the transfer happen. I had been on the phone with them for the past hour trying to get more information on when the money would be in the account. The lady finally told me that the funds had been approved and that the money should be available in the next seventy-two hours at the most. I thanked the lady who had given me the status update and disconnected the call.

I felt like I was making some progress. I sat in my room wondering if I should tell Dread that I was carrying his child. I also contemplated telling him where I was going. I already had it worked out in my head that he could continue his music career in Atlanta. Lucky Lamar was his ticket into the music scene there and he could record as much as he wanted once we got settled. That was the easiest part of my plan. The hard part was telling him that I was pregnant and it was his baby. I wasn't sure how he would process that information. I figured it was now or never though. He could reject my idea of him coming south with us or he could embrace the idea. Either way, I was going to Atlanta and starting my life over. I just hoped he wanted to start a life with me.

I gathered myself and figured I should start packing up all of my belongings scattered about the room. I had kept the maids from coming inside my room because I know some of those shady bitches got sticky fingers. All it would take is for them to find out I had large amounts of cash in the room before they tried to help themselves to a pay raise. I didn't see any reason to stay there another night. I had the confirmation I needed about our money. We could leave. We had more than enough cash on hand to make the trip to Georgia, and get settled. I needed to let Neko know that the money would be in my account in a few days and that we could push. I hadn't really seen him much over the last three days. I was sure he was in his room freaking.

The walls in the run down hole in the wall were thin, so I could hear his late night escapades. He would stop over to my room to check on me every now and again to make sure "we" were ok. It was fine by me that he left me alone because I was frustrated and didn't want to take it out on him.

This day was different though. I could almost see the light at the end of the tunnel. We would be headed 85 South real soon and away from all of the chaotic bullshit in DC. I perked up just thinking about not having to look over my shoulder every time I went out to the ice machine or to the store for snacks. I would be free of worrying about my "so called" sister trying to take my head off.

I decided to shower and get out of the room. I needed to get the conversation with Dread over with. There was no need to prolong it anymore. Either he was coming or he was not. Either he wanted the baby and to be a part of my life or he didn't. No matter how it played out, I owed it to him to know he had a choice in some of everything that was going on. He deserved that much. I couldn't see having a baby and not at least giving the father the option of being in the child's life. I rummaged through my bags and found a pair of *Love Pink* sweatpants and a plain white t-shirt. I pulled my hair into a ponytail and headed out of the door.

I was feeling better than I had in the past two days. I guess having some clarity could do that for you. I knocked on Neko's room door. He didn't answer. I knocked harder. I could finally hear him moving about the room. When the door opened I was shocked that it wasn't Neko. It was female who was wrapped in a towel. She was obviously in the middle of a shower and I had disturbed her.

"Um, is Neko here?" I asked

The girl had the nerve to cock an attitude. She crossed her arms across her large chest and rolled her eyes. "Yeah, he's here. Who are you?" She demanded snapping her neck and rolling her beady little eyes.

I just smiled and tried to remain civil. I really wanted to smack her for trying to be cute. "I'm his sister. Can you tell him that I have to step out and I will be back in a few hours."

The girl looked like she didn't believe me. "How I know you are really his sister?" She asked me in a huffy tone.

"If I wasn't his sister I would have beat the shit out of you if I would have caught you in there with my man." I said pointing into the room. "Just let him know I will be back and that he should be ready to make some moves when I come back. Can you handle delivering that message or should I write it down for you? You can read can't you?" I shot back. I was trying to rile the stupid bitch up since she wanted to get cute.

She looked like she wanted to say something else, but I didn't even give her the chance. I put my hand up in her face to stop her.

"Make sure you give him the message and be gone when I come back because you don't want it with me for real." I said chuckling. She just didn't know I would punish her little ass.

I walked away from the dumbfounded broad standing in the doorway and proceeded down the steps to the car. I could hear her young dumb ass fussing and cursing at Neko as I got in the car. I sent Neko a message letting him know I would be back and that he should be ready to leave in the morning.

I knew he probably had his hands full with his big-breasted female friend, and he wasn't going to get the message until he could calm her down. I decided I wanted to buy a few things for the road. I went to a *Walmart* that was located further up the street. I bought a cooler and some new luggage. I got the kind that had a lock on it. I wanted to transfer the money we had in cash into the luggage and lock it away inside. I wanted to pull out of DC looking like we were going on vacation rather than looking like we were fleeing.

I bought a few personal items too and stopped to look in the beauty section. I had never shopped in *Walmart*. It wasn't exactly my normal style, but I couldn't help grabbing up some hair dye. I would change my whole appearance, hair color and all. I may as well switch it up. I was moving to a new area, I might as well change what I look like too. I picked out a spicy cinnamon color. I walked through the baby aisle and could not move from there. I looked around at all the bottles and booties. I looked at the blankets and all of the things I was going to have to purchase when I got to Atlanta.

I started to wonder what I had created. Was it a girl or boy? Would it be healthy? Would I be a good mother? Then it hit me. I wasn't supposed to be shopping I was supposed to be leaving so I could live long enough to know what I would be having. I pushed the cart down the aisle and headed to the register to pay for my items. I paid for my things and left. As I got in the car, I started making one of my last trips across the Woodrow Wilson Bridge. I didn't have to put any thought into where I was headed. I crossed the bridge and headed up 295 to the Southside.

It was time. It was time for me to tell Dread. I couldn't stall or conceal this secret from him anymore. I had too many other little secrets, but this one was different. I couldn't keep it from him. I found myself parked in front of his building again. My palms were sweaty and I was nervous. No matter how much I had prepared myself for our needed conversation, I really wasn't ready to have it. I sat there fighting the urge to say fuck it, crank up the engine, leave and never look back. I felt like I was chained to the seat. I can't explain why I didn't just go in there and tell him; instead I sat there in what felt like the safety of my car. No one knew I had switched rides. The windows were tinted just enough so no one could see inside. I fumbled through my purse and found a pen and a piece of paper. I wrote Dread a letter instead.

Dear Dread,

There are so many things I want to tell you. I know the circumstances surrounding my life may have complicated what could have been. I will understand if after you read this, you never want to speak to or see me again.

I have been careless and wreckless my entire life. I have lived carefree and done many things I am not proud of; however, after meeting you I may have found a reason to stay on the straight and narrow.

I have finally decided on heading south. I know you aren't ready to leave your life here in DC behind, but you have created a life within me. I found out I am pregnant. This is a lot to take in, I know. I could not keep this from you. Every child deserves the right to know his or her parents. I hope you can forgive me for telling you this way, but I could not face you to tell you this. I couldn't take either sadness or rejection. Nor could I take you being the man I think you are and face you if you were happy about this life we have created together.

I am putting the ball in your court. I will contact you once I make it to Georgia. By then, I pray that you have digested all I have told you and make a decision on what could be the start of something beautiful.

Love Always,
YaYa

I finished the letter and folded it. I knew if I second guessed myself, I would chicken out and not take it to his door. I walked out into the courtyard with my head down, hoping no one, including Dread, would pay me any attention. I slipped inside his building and up the steps. I crept the whole way. I felt like my heart was beating so hard it would burst through my chest. Once I reached his door, I swallowed hard. It was now or never. I could knock and tell him face to face or I could slide the note under the door to his apartment and haul ass down the steps and push it back across the bridge, grab my brother and get the fuck out of the DMV. I decided on the latter of the two and quietly slide the letter under the door and silently made my way back down the steps. I never looked back. I walked straight out of the front door and had to stop myself from making a run for it to the car. Instead, I walked briskly to the car like I had somewhere to be and got in the car and got out of there as fast as I could.

I blew through the stop sign at the end of the block. My heart rate didn't return to semi-normal until I got to the mouth of the Wilson Bridge. I took the first exit across the bridge and pulled into the first place I saw. I was shaking and breathing heavy like I had run across the bridge instead of driven. I got out and threw up. *This pregnancy shit was going to be rough.*

I didn't even see them. I never heard the car pull in behind me. I was too busy trying to control my nerves. I felt the blow to my back first. Before I could even comprehend that someone was hurting me, I felt fists raining down on me. Blow after blow until I fell to the ground. I curled up into a ball and tried to protect my stomach. When I tried to do that, whoever was attacking me began to kick me in my chest, and face until everything faded to black.

CHAPTER 31

The room around me was dark as I gained consciousness. Restraints bound my hands and legs, containing me; upright, in a chair. I screamed out into the darkness. To no avail. I could hear something moving above me. My guess was that I was in a basement. I could feel something moving around my ankles. Fear overtook me. I tried frantically to get myself out of my restraints. My body was in incredible pain from the beating I had sustained. My upper body was beaten and bruised.. I wanted to scream again, but I decided against it. Whoever had attacked me was somewhere nearby. I had to try and get myself out of what felt like those plastic ties that the police used to keep suspects from moving.

I wiggled every way I could, trying not to fall over in the chair I was bound to. It was useless. I wasn't getting out of those restraints. I was panicking. I could hear the footsteps above me moving around again, they sounded like they were getting closer. A door opened, and I heard heels clinking down what sounded like wooden steps. The person was approaching from behind, so I could not see who it was. I tensed up knowing that whoever it was meant me no good.

I know it was her. She had found me. I tried to strain my neck to see who it was. A mixture of curiosity and fear washed over me. I wanted to know who she was. I also wanted whoever it was to let me live.

The mystery woman stopped inches behind me. Her presence, coupled with my vulnerability; made the hair on the back of my neck stand up. I could smell her perfume. It was familiar. I couldn't quite place it, but I knew the scent.

"Who are you?" I asked in a weak tone. "Look, if it is money you want, you can have it all. Just don't hurt me!" I pleaded.

Nothing. She didn't respond. Instead I could hear her walk away to the far corner of the room. The light came on and I blinked trying to focus on anything. I was looking to see if I could recognize where I was. I saw what had been crawling around by my ankles and feet. It was rats. They scattered all about when the lights were turned on. I wish I were with them. I wish I could run and hide with them.

The fresh tears formed at the corners of my eyes. I started to babble. "Please don't hurt me. I'm pregnant!" I cried. I heard the heels come up behind me fast. She grabbed my hair and yanked my head backwards.

"I don't give a fuck about you or that bitch ass baby of yours." She laughed.

I couldn't believe whose voice I was hearing. It was NiQue.

She had twisted my hair into her fist. She yanked me backwards, harder this time. We were eye to eye for the first time. I could see the hatred in her eyes. I knew she was mad, but I didn't think she was mad enough to go as far as she was going.

"NiQue, I know we haven't been ourselves lately. We can work this shit out." I tried to reason.

She let my hair go and walked in front of me. She didn't look at me, she stared through me. "I have never been myself YaYa." Her face was blank. She looked crazed. I didn't know what the fuck she was talking about.

"That's the problem, I don't know who the fuck I am. For years I thought I was NiQue. Then I found out that was far from the truth." She blinked as if she were trying to get a grip on reality. "It is amazing how relaxed people are when they think their skeletons are hidden deep in the closet. Until...someone uncovers a few bones." She said.

"What bones? NiQue we talk about everything?" I was trying to talk her off of the deep end. I didn't know what planet she was visiting, but it damn sure wasn't Earth.

"You are used to getting whatever you want. Whatever nigga, whatever car, and whatever YaYa wants...she gets!" She suddenly screamed. "Now, I am gonna get what I want." Her voice had returned to that airy spacey sounding tone.

"NiQue, I don't know what is wrong with you, but if this is about Dread, you can have him. Ain't no nigga worth this shit. I thought we vowed never to let a nigga come between us." I said boldly hoping that she would let me go.

She turned her back to me and began laughing. "You are so fucking stupid YaSheema! This has nothing to do with you giving him to me, although, I will have him when I am through with you." She said wickedly. She turned around and she was holding a box cutter. I was praying that she was going to use it to free me from my restraints. I had feeling that she had other plans though. Her eyes had gone back to the wild-eyed, glazed-over, drugged-up look from before. She was there, but she wasn't *all there* mentally. I couldn't help but think that the drugs she had been shoveling into her system over the years had finally fucked her up.

"Look NiQue, whatever you're mad about, we can work this shit out." I said, never taking my eyes off of the box cutter in her hands.

"I want to tell you a little story." NiQue said.

She backed up from me and retrieved a chair from the far left corner of the dank basement. She pulled the chair along with her until it was positioned right in front of me. She retracted the blade on the box cutter and let it fall in her lap. I started to calm down a bit when she put her weapon down, but I was still on edge because she still had the upper hand. She started doing that stare through me thing again and I knew NiQue had left the building. At least mentally.

"Once upon a time there was a little girl named NiQue" She started. Her voice had changed to that of a little girl. I couldn't believe the bitch was as crazy as she was. Her eyes were red and they were fixated on me. I got the feeling she was looking through instead of at me. She was actually going to sit there and tell me a story. I sat quietly though, because I wasn't sure how crazy NiQue really was. She might really try and harm me. I kept my eyes on the box cutter in her lap and tried to pay attention to what she was trying to say to me.

"ShaNiqua grew up with her brother in Northeast, DC. Her brother took care of her as best as he could, until one day NiQue found out that her brother wasn't her brother. She was supposed to be out shopping with her best friend, but instead she had stayed home. Unknown to NiQue's brother, NiQue was in her room with her ear pressed to the vent listening to a very important conversation. This was her way of learning all that she could about her brother's business ties, by spying on his conversations.

It was a conversation about money. There was nothing abnormal about that since that NiQue had heard her brother argue about who owed him cash on more than one occasion. But that time was different though. The conversation ShaNiqua's brother was having was more about blackmail. He knew something, and the person he was talking to did not want anyone else knowing the information her brother was aware of. Needless to say, no one knew NiQue heard the conversation until many moons later.

Because of her eavesdropping, NiQue found out that her brother was not her brother ,but a paid imposter. He had no blood ties to NiQue at all. She also found out that the stories he had told her growing up about her mother and father were untrue. Just a fabrication from a paid imposter. She learned many things that day with her ear pressed firmly against that vent. She learned that her whole fucking life was a lie!

NiQue held in what she had learned for a very long time, not wanting it to be the truth. She held on to the things she heard until one day while having an argument with her "brother" she snapped. She told him that she knew he was not her real brother and that he was paid to be her babysitter and the keeper of the truth.

At first her brother denied it, but NiQue let him know that her real father was rich beyond her imagination, that she had heard the argument about money, and that there was nothing he could do to stop her from confronting her Dad about what she had found out. Well, to make a long story short, she confronted her father and he rejected her. He denied all of the questions she asked. This enraged NiQue and it made her angry and spiteful. She wanted to know why her father could love one of his children but not the other.

NiQue harbored ill feelings for the man who helped give her life. She dug up as much information as she could on who she was, and low and behold she found out not only did she have a sister, but a brother too. YaYa, do you see where I am going with this?" She asked cutting her story short. She looked at me trying to see if I was following the story.

My mouth was wide open. I knew what she was saying even though she had not said it yet. She was *Pajay*. I was too stunned to speak. I just nodded my head up and down. I didn't want to do anything that might cause her to attack.

"You see Daddy dearest knocked your gutter ass mother up

and mine too. He decided since Christa beat my mother to the punch with telling him that she was pregnant he would keep her junkie ass instead. He dropped my mother like she was nothing and continued to cater to Christa. Apparently, after I was born my mother could not handle the pressures of raising a baby on her own. She left me on my father's doorstep and from what I could find out she killed herself. She was already ashamed for getting knocked up by her sister's man! She couldn't handle the rejection.

Instead of him raising me as his child, he paid one of his goons to play Daddy. They set it up that his goon would act as my brother and take care of me as long as Daddy paid the bills and made sure I didn't need anything. What Daddy didn't know is that my "so called" big brother had a thing for young virginal pussy. He raped and molested me every chance he got, which was often, because he was all I knew and all I had. He would threaten me and tell me things like, Child Protective Service would take me away and that bad things would happen to me if I told anyone what he was doing to me.

I kept it all to myself, afraid that I would lose my brother. The only family I thought I had, not knowing that he wasn't my brother at all. He was just a paid child molester employed by my father to keep me out of his hair while he played Daddy to you. Then I heard that conversation, the one that changed everything. I was disgusted that my father didn't want me. He left me. He let a grown ass man rape me over and over so he could make his precious YaYa comfortable, while he left me in hell to fend for myself."

I could not believe any of the shit I was hearing. She had to be making that shit up. There was no way that Daddy would leave his children out there by themselves. It just didn't make any sense. I finally responded to her version of events.

"There is no way Daddy would have left one of his children behind like that. I don't believe you NiQue!" I said.

She began to laugh hysterically. "What do you mean he wouldn't do it? What do you think he did to Neko? He knew about him. He never tried to even take him off the streets. He just let Christa ruin the boy. He didn't give a fuck about Neko or me! All he cared about was your ass." She said getting heated all over again.

I wasn't trying to upset her, but it was a lot to take in. I was trying to make sense of it all and that was like finding a needle in a haystack. The key players weren't around to question about the moves they had made. They were all dead. NiQue stood up and took a few steps closer to me. She held the box cutter in her hands. The blade was still retracted.

"You see, Daddy never anticipated me finding out about his lies and betrayal. He just thought that he could keep paying my "brother" to raise me and all would be fine. He didn't think I would figure out that it was a lie. After the conversation he and Mike had about getting more money to keep Daddy's dirty secret, I waited until Mike left out of the house and went through all of his shit.

I went through everything I could get my hands on to see if there was anything left behind who I really was. Then I found it. I found my birth certificate listing Darnell Clayton as the father and Donna Reynolds as the mother to one baby girl born on November 17, 1986. I knew it was mine because they never switched up my birth date. They just changed my name to ShaniQua Watkins to match Mike's last name. My mother had named me Pajay Clayton."

I was trembling in my chair. I was trying to wrap my mind around all of the information NiQue was laying on me. Not only had Daddy hidden Neko from me, he was sleeping with Christa's baby sister, Donna. That was the reason he had hidden NiQue. Not because he didn't want her, but because of the affair he was having with Momma's sister. My head was spinning. I couldn't believe that because of the generational mistakes our parents had made, my unborn child and I were the ones who were paying for it. I was floored at all of the things she was telling me. My head was swimming. I was confused. I didn't even know what to call her.

"NiQue, did you kill Daddy and did you say, 'Donna Reynolds' as in my mother's sister?" I asked her wanting clarification.

She laughed a psychotic laugh. "But of course I killed his trifling ass! He had to go! When I confronted him, he pushed me away and told me he would kill me if I told anyone about his infidelities. So, like any Clayton, it was kill or be killed. He had to go! You had already done me the favor of getting rid of that whore of a mother of yours. I actually owe you one for that. I didn't even have to get my hands dirty fucking with her."

She was walking around the chair in a circle like a mad dog. "Just so you know, your shit is fucked up too. Your father was fucking your aunt and your mother. I am your sister and your cousin!" She laughed. She was getting a kick out of making me sick.

I just sat dumfounded. There was nothing else I could do. My stomach started to turn. She was going to kill me and there was nothing I could do to stop her. She had the upper hand. My mind thought back to all the times we went out and did our dirt. Then it hit me like a ton of bricks. I had slept with that crazy bitch! I had actually laid down with her and we had had sex! I had fucked my own sister!

"NiQue, did you know all of this before we slept together? I mean, did you know we shared a father before we had sex?" I questioned.

She continued to walk around my chair in circles laughing. "Of course I knew you were my sister by then. I just wanted to see how you would treat me afterwards. I wanted you to accept me. I knew you got down with girls from time to time. Hell, you told me yourself that you and Corrine had done the nasty. I just wanted to know if you could accept and love me the way I wanted to be loved. All I wanted was my family to love me and treat me the way

I was supposed to be treated."

I threw up all over myself just thinking about what she was telling me. I knew there was something unnatural about the sex that night. It wasn't because it was with a chick, but it was because I was with my fucking sister!

"How could you do that to me NiQue!" I screamed.

"Stop fucking calling me that! My name is Pajay Clayton! You will address me as Pajay from now on!" She yelled back at me.

She cocked her head to the side and laughed. "Actually, you don't have that long to live, so it really doesn't matter." She taunted.

"Oh my god, did you kill Corrine?" I asked through my sobs.

"Let me hip you to a lot of shit big sis. I owe you the truth since you are gonna die anyway! I set you up over and over again. Each time you managed to get out of the shit – I don't know how you managed to do it, but you did – from Papi finding you in the club the night we met Dread, to the day Corrine died. It was supposed to be you each and every time. You are just lucky as shit. Papi was sloppy with his own shit. He was caught up in some other shit. Were you really that stupid that you couldn't see that I was always nowhere to be found when someone was gunning for you?"

I wanted to kick her ass, but there was no way out of the restraints to do so. She knew if it hadn't been for the restraints I would have been all over her ass. "It was you who killed Daddy and Oscar, but why did you kill Oscar; NiQue?" I asked making a mistake and calling her by her made-up name.

She slid the box cutter to full length and grabbed my throat. "I killed that old bag Oscar because he knew I was Darnell's daughter the whole time. He stood by and let this shit happen. He knew it wasn't right. Jew Jew and Timmie tried to take him out when they killed our bitch ass Daddy, but he didn't die. So, I had to make a special trip to the hospital and see to it that he didn't ruin my surprise. If it helps you feel any better, he died peacefully. A pillow over the face while under the influence of pain medications just may be the best way to die." She chuckled at a joke that was clearly not funny to anyone but her. I sat there shaking my head back and forth. I couldn't believe she was so calm and calculated about killing people.

"NiQue, Oscar didn't deserve to die!" I said crying.

I thought I just told you not to call me NiQue you dumb bitch!" She said holding the blade right up against my throat. Her face was so close to mine I could smell her hatred for me.

"I'm sorry." I tried to say, but it was too late. She sliced into the left side of my. I could feel the open cut and the blood pouring from it. I refused to give her the satisfaction of screaming anymore. Anything she gave me, I was going to take it like a soldier. She let me go. I wanted to reach up and touch my face to stop the blood from pouring out of the cut.

"You were like family to me Pajay. How could you do this to me? I did nothing but love you?" I said trying to get her to talk so I could at least know why she had done all of the horrible things to the people I cared about the most.

"You didn't fuck with me. As soon as you got the chance, you fucked the nigga I wanted. I even gave you another chance by fucking you, trying to make you love me and you carried me again. I have to admit, you almost got away from me too.

I had everyone looking for you. Caesar tried to get you to come in to meet with him and you didn't show. I didn't know where you had gone until I started to watch Dread's house and you showed up there. I almost gave up on finding you, but true to my bloodline I stayed on my mission!" She said proudly sticking her chest out.

"Pajay, Neko and I didn't do anything to hurt you. We don't deserve to die. You got who you needed to get. Just let us go!" I said forgetting that I wasn't going to beg her for anything, including my life. I was pleading for the life of my unborn and for my brother who didn't deserve her shit.

"Who said anything about hurting Neko? If I wanted to harm him I could have a long time ago. He was living with me remember? Or were you too busy fucking my man to even care? I could have taken him out when I killed my "so called brother" Mike. Neko is safe because he is innocent and caught up in this mess just like I was. He was lied to. He never knew who his father was until I wanted it known! You on the other hand, are a whole different story!"

She got eerily quiet. As long as she was talking I felt calm. It was when she stopped talking that I became nervous. It was definite that she wasn't going to let me live. I started to think that all the dirt I had done was going to come back on me full circle. I was paying for all my sins. I was paying for the sins of others. I knew I was about to join my mother, Papi and the countless others I had hurt. We stared each other down. I was searching her face for some type of resemblance to our family. Maybe she looked more like the aunt I had never met. I couldn't be sure. I was looking for signs of Daddy in her face. It was obvious she was one of us. It didn't matter if she looked like us or not. She was as ruthless as any of us, and that alone was enough proof for me.

I felt the overwhelming urge to want to hug her and tell her that she didn't have to go through with any of what she was planning. I wanted to make things right with her. Neither one of us were perfect. As a matter of fact, we were both fucked up. *DNA is a mother fucker!* Our corrupt upbringing turned us into killers, and our parental influence taught us to have no regard for human life. Our genetics had us mentally unstable and that instability made us not have a care for who we hurt. Our common bond was murder; not our parents. Who was I to blame NiQue for her hatred towards Daddy? I hated Momma just the same for leaving me and never being the mother I wanted her to be. I smiled to myself just thinking about how everything would play out.

"What the fuck are you smiling about?" NiQue asked.

"I just wanted to tell you that I love you NiQue and that I am sorry." I whispered. "I apologize for whatever you went through, and I wish we could have figured out a better way of dealing with all of this." I said.

NiQue or Pajay, or whoever she was at that moment, pounced on me. She was slashing at my face, arms, and neck. I couldn't even defend myself because I was still tied to the chair. She was screaming about her name not being NiQue, and that is when I felt the box cutter rip through my abdomen and I knew there was no more baby and no more reason for me to live anymore.

As my eyes fluttered closed, I saw everyone I had missed so much. They were beckoning to me to join them. My father, mother, and Oscar were all there waiting for me. I even saw Papi and Corrine waving for me to come to them. They all wore huge smiles; I could tell they were happy they were free and I knew I would be too. Through the pain of her stabbing me repeatedly, I was oddly happy to know I could stop running, and that is just what I did.

CHAPTER 32

Dread

It was late in the evening when I finally got out of the bed to head to the studio. Imagine how surprised I was to find a note from YaYa on the floor of my apartment where it looked like she had slid it up under the door. I read the note and immediately called her to tell her that I would go with her. If for no other reason, I would go for my seed. She never answered. I called her for three days straight. I thought she was playing games with me until a detective showed up at my door, three weeks later, to ask me a few questions. He wanted to know if I knew anything about the murder of YaSheema Marie Clayton.

That cracker mutha fucka had the nerve to insinuate that I may have killed her because she was pregnant and the baby was mine. That bamma had the nerve to say I was the number one suspect! I tried to let the asshole Gatsby know that I had just found out that she was carrying my baby the day she went missing; but he wasn't trying to hear it. They had found her body sliced up really bad. She was tied to a chair and dumped by Blue Plains.

What was I supposed to say to Detective Gatsby besides I didn't know what the fuck happened? YaYa was tangled up in so much drama, I didn't think they would ever know who did it. It saddened me because ole' girl had a nigga's heart from the moment I met her; not to mention she was carrying my baby. All a nigga could do was pray for her soul. It really took me some time to get over that shit with the loss of her and my baby, but to my surprise, NiQue really helped me out. She was right there for me while I grieved. She was the reason the detective left me alone about the whole thing. She gave him a statement saying I was with her the night YaYa disappeared. I didn't expect shorty to even fuck with me after I had told her we couldn't get down like that because I was really feeling YaYa. She played her position as my friend and gave me my space while I mourned what would have been my first born.

Funny how shit changes. NiQue and I are seeing each other and she turned out to be a straight rider. I see why she and YaYa were friends. She held me down when I didn't even want to deal with anyone. She gave me my space and helped me make it through the funeral for YaYa. In the beginning, I felt bad for dating her after all that had happened to YaYa. In a weird sort of way she reminded me of her and she was the only thing I had left to remind me of YaYa. NiQue and I are planning to get married before the end of the summer and she is expecting our baby girl any day now. NiQue suggested we name her YaSheema Nicole. I wasn't so sure that that would be a good idea, but she insisted. Who am I to argue? I am just excited about having a healthy, baby girl.

YaYa's little brother Neko, has been throwing all kinds of shade my way since his sister's funeral. I guess I would be scrutinizing any and everybody too in order to find out what happened to my peoples. He and I exchanged a few words at YaYa's funeral, and he even let NiQue and I know in so many words, that he didn't approve of our marriage. He feels like it is disrespectful. I know this shit is crazy how it all happened, but I am rolling with the punches at this point. There is nothing I can do for the love I lost or for my seed. I can only move forward at this point and support my soon to be wife and my daughter. Sometimes, I wish things could have been different, but you can't change God's plan. What is meant for you is specifically meant for you. That's how I look at it. I try not to dwell on the past. I try to focus on the future. Although, it saddens me to think of YaYa and my baby, I wish I would have had more time with her. I know deep down she was supposed to be "the one" from the first day I met her. I still smile thinking of the day we met. My record, "No City for Old Men" is due to drop by the end of the summer. Even though NiQue doesn't know it, my song, "Exclusive" was created for YaSheema.

CHAPTER 33

Neko Reynolds

I couldn't figure out what happened to YaYa that day. I wish I would have never let that silly bitch I had been fucking in my hotel room answer the door. Had she not been there, things may have gone down differently. Maybe my sister would still be alive had I answered the door myself.

I have had a million, "what ifs" since they found YaYa's body. I haven't been able to cope. All I have left is NiQue. We have been thick as thieves since this shit has happened and I don't know what I would have done without her. She is getting ready to get married and she's expecting her first baby with that nigga Dread. I ain't really feeling their union because I think he had something to do with my sister's death. I can tell you one thing; I ain't gonna rest until I find out what happened to my sister. That's for damn sure. She was all I had left.

The money that Pop left us hit YaYa's account the day after she went missing, and I ended up being over two million dollars richer. The crazier shit about that is that whoever that "Pajay" person is collected her money from Pop's insurance and I haven't heard shit from her since. Odd ain't it?

A few weeks after they found YaYa, they found my mother's body. It had washed up in the Potomac. The media was in frenzy over that shit because they kept making wild assumptions, saying my sister killed my Mother and Father. They ended up deeming Oscar's death a homicide and tried to pin that shit on my sister too! Since they pinned all of it on my sister, it cleared my name and I was free to do as I pleased. Needless to say, I never left the city. I stayed right here in DC. I opened up my car detailing shop and I am making more money than I could have possibly imagined. I am doing it the legit way too!

My life has been crazy since the day I met my father and sister. I have been trying to dead this nagging feeling that shit ain't what it really seems. I know the answers to my questions rest with both my sisters. I got the sinking feeling Dread got something he ain't telling either. Until I can find Pajay, I may never find out the truth. I can tell you one thing though; I got the best detective on the case to find out who and where she is.

Detective Gatsby seems hell bent on finding out what happened to my sister and finding this mystery sister even if it is the last thing he does. He seems to be sure that there is a piece missing from the puzzle. He feels like this nigga Dread got something to do with it too! For his sake, he better hope I never find out he hurt my sister or he will fully understand our family reputation.

CHAPTER 34

NiQue Watkins/Pajay Reynolds

I guess the best bitches won in the end. We had to put on our poker face so no one would know we had anything to do with what had happened to our dearly departed best friend and sister. We even cried at YaYa's funeral! If you ask NiQue, YaYa got just what she deserved. If you ask Pajay, we have no regrets! As long as Neko and Dread continue to do right by us, I guess I will let them live.

Neko isn't really feeling the fact that we are about to have a baby with Dread, but the heart wants what the heart wants. Besides, he was ours first! Our whore of a sister bedded him and got pregnant, and we almost lost him because of that shit! I don't think our brother is going to show up at the wedding at the end of the month. He better not do anything to ruin our special day! He just can't seem to get over YaYa. I have tried everything to make shit right between us. We even asked him to be the one to give us away at the wedding and he declined!

One thing for certain though, that fucking Detective Gatsby has been snooping around lately and if he knows what's good for him he better stay out of our path! Fucking with us could lead him to an early retirement. Now if you will excuse us, we haven't been feeling well today, and I swear I hope that I have this baby soon because we hate this pregnancy shit! We didn't want a fucking kid anyway…but if that is what Dread wants, then that is what he will get. As long as he keeps loving us, we ain't got any problems!

THE END????

Stay Tuned
for
Dirty DNA 2: Til Death Do Us Part

G STREET CHRONICLES
~ PRESENTS ~

How Do You
Survive In A World
That Has Turned
It's Back On You?

Exhale

A Short Story

BLAQUE

Exhale

A Short Story

BLAQUE

Butterfii Fields has been through it all in her young life from watching her teenage mother being physically and mentally abused to being impregnated by her own father. She has been raped and tortured. She no longer trusts anyone but the siblings who endured the same abuse as she. Years of abuse have led the fragile Butterflii to commit the ultimate crime, murder. She is deemed mentally unstable and her crime lands her in the infamous mental hospital St. Elizabeth's in S.E. Washington, DC where she meets the only person she feels she has a connection to, Georgia Marks.

Georgia, the complete opposite of Butterflii, is beautiful and smart and seems to have everything under control, except one thing, her drug problem. Georgia battles her own demons which stems from a past of her abuse of the drug, Love Boat that runs rampant through the DMV streets at an all time high.

Her addiction to the powerful drug LB, the death of her brother Emilio accompanied by a heist gone wrong places Georgia in St. Elizabeth's.

Together, they break free from bondage and develop something they have never felt for anyone…love. The two girls embark on a journey to find themselves and make a way to survive in a world that has shunned and turned its back on them, only to find the bond they thought could never be broken will be, by a twist of fate that will devastate the unsuspecting Butterflii who refuses to forgive.

G STREET CHRONICLES
SHORT STORY EBOOKS

We'd like to thank you for supporting G Street Chronicles and invite you to join our social networks. Please be sure to post a review when you're finished reading.

Facebook
G Street Chronicles
&
G Street Chronicles CEO Exclusive Readers Group

Twitter
@GStreetChronicl

My Space
G Street Chronicles

Email us and we'll add you to our mailing list
fans@gstreetchronicles.com

George Sherman Hudson, CEO
Shawna A., VP